THE LURE OF ADVENTURE . . .

From the lusty court of Queen Bess to the treasure-laden jungles of the New World, Shawn MacManus pursued adventure, fortune, and a treacherous Spanish beauty, Doña Elvira. . . .

"Inside my own chamber I bolted the door, kicked off my boots and fumbled in my rucksack for a nightshirt. It was then that the curtains on the four-poster stirred faintly. Even in the dance of the candle end, there was no mistaking the head and shoulders that were thrust out to greet me.

" 'Where have you been, *novio mío?*' asked Elvira. 'I thought you were never coming!' "

THE GOLDEN ONES
was originally published by Hanover House.

Books by Frank G. Slaughter

Published by POCKET BOOKS

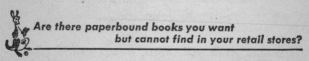

Frank G. Slaughter

THE GOLDEN ONES

*(Published originally
under the pseudonym
C. V. Terry)*

PUBLISHED BY POCKET BOOKS NEW YORK

THE GOLDEN ONES

Doubleday edition published 1957

POCKET BOOK edition published August, 1958
4th printing.........................May, 1976

This POCKET BOOK edition includes every word contained in the original, higher-priced edition. It is printed from brand-new plates made from completely reset, clear, easy-to-read type.
POCKET BOOK editions are published by
POCKET BOOKS,
a division of Simon & Schuster, Inc.,
A GULF+WESTERN COMPANY
630 Fifth Avenue,
New York, N.Y. 10020.
Trademarks registered in the United States and other countries.

ISBN: 0-671-80544-4.

Contents

CHAPTER I

The Swan and Dolphin

MOST OF us have opened our eyes in strange beds and wondered what brought us there. That autumn dawn I had wakened abruptly, in full possession of my senses. I knew that I lay in a chamber at the Swan and Dolphin, an inn on the highroad to London Town; I recalled precisely how I had come here and why. But I needed a full heartbeat before I could name my bedfellow—a lovely wench indeed, who still slept beside me in an attitude that could only be described as abandoned.

The sequence of events that had resulted in this enticing proximity were crystal clear. We had met only yesterday outside Oxford. The lady's coach had been stranded with a broken spring; it had been but natural to pause and offer my services. . . . The ensuing game of thrust-and-parry (to use a fencing term) had been no less forthright—but the real reason for her appearance in my bed still teased my curiosity. It would be false modesty to deny that I am a man of parts. But I could not quite believe that Elvira Moreno y Quesada had appeared there solely from admiration of my person.

Elvira (if that was her true name) continued to sleep like a contented kitten. Her full red lips were smiling at a dream in which I could only hope that I was the chief performer. I disengaged my arm gently, without disturbing her repose. At this moment, with all desire slaked, it was easy to view her with the eyes of a cynic. Even so, I found that the pearl light of dawn did nothing to diminish her freshness. Wise though it had proved in the ancient arts of love-making, there was something almost virginal about the body that nested so trustingly against my own.

I have tumbled my share of women—and some were comely wildcats indeed. None could match my present bedmate: I repeated this conviction soberly as I continued to admire her with the eyes of a connoisseur. From its firm-fleshed thighs (so opulent, for all their apparent slenderness) to those twin doves of Venus with their rock-hard nipples, this was a body made for love, a lyre where a man might play any tune he fancied. Only a credulous boy would imagine he had been the first to waken that instrument to such perfect harmonies—and I was a boy no longer.

The woman had pursued me to this refuge: no one could call me her seducer. Of course, it was quite possible that Señorita Moreno y Quesada was the noble lady she seemed, the niece of the grandee who had ridden beside her in the coach (and had disappeared so conveniently after our arrival at the inn). Even in far-off Cork, I had heard that the court of Elizabeth Tudor was licentious beyond belief. When she had opened my chamber door Doña Elvira might simply have availed herself of the morals of her milieu—taking her bed sport where she found it, as casually as another, more decorous damsel might filch sweetmeats from the sideboard.

It was a happy conceit—and I played with it a moment more, if only to soothe my self-esteem. Another part of my mind (shall I call it common sense?) insisted that I must pay a price for my dalliance, that the bill would be presented in due course. Until my siren wakened, I had no way of knowing what that price would be.

Perhaps I should pause here (as it were, on the threshold of my narrative), even as I paused on London's doorsill in that autumn dawn of 1594, to introduce myself more fully. Know you, then, that I am called Sean MacManus (the English spell it Shawn). Must I add that I am an Irishman, with enough Scottish blood in my veins to temper recklessness with caution?

Although not of the nobility, I can claim—against any disputant—to be of gentle birth. My mother was a Barry (there is no finer family in all Ireland). My father, though a farmer, served for a time as queen's magistrate in our district. My mother and I were always close; I respected, and even admired, her husband, though I had no real affection for him. Alfred MacManus and I had few interests in common. So little were our natures joined, there were times when I told myself (as is the nature of youth the world over) that this solemn countryman was not my real father, that the pensive look in my mother's eyes had a genesis far removed from Cork.

Though there was no love lost between us, my father never stinted me in matters pertaining to the rights of an Irish gentleman. There was always a tutor in our household—and, thanks to this dry-as-chalk fellow, I soon acquired the ability to write the "secretary hand" favored by most clerks. I was no Latinist, but I could parse in both Spanish and French. Mathematics was a science I found congenial; though I had yet to put my knowledge to the test, I was confident that I could navigate the Ocean Sea with astrolabe and quadrant. . . . Irishmen come naturally by such pursuits as riding, hunting, and fighting with shillelagh and claymore, so I needed no particular schooling in such fields. Thanks to my massive frame (I stand six feet two in my hose) I excelled in them all from childhood.

My father (if he *was* my father) died just before I attained my majority. Since he had been married before, with a healthy, hulking son as issue, I was given no share of his estate. My mother, who had been in failing health for years, was grudgingly allowed to remain in the manor house on the River Lee. The right had been granted her in her husband's will: though I cordially disliked the new master of the manse, I had lingered to comfort her last days on earth.

There was nothing to hold me in Ireland after her death. My half brother had brought out this fact, just before I gave him two black eyes and a broken nose as final tokens of my regard. So it was with no regret whatever, and a certain pleasure of accomplishment, that I set out to seek my fortune in London.

My ruling passion had always been the drama: it was my firm intention to carve out a career as playwright in that burgeoning field. My tutor (who held a degree from Oxford and had once lived in London) had advised me to seek out Master Richard Burbage, director of the famous theater outside the city walls, where plays and spectacles were offered almost daily. Could I but secure a place as apprentice in his company (said my pedagogue) I would find it an ideal climate to woo the muses.

Casting my mind ahead as I voyaged across the Irish Sea to Liverpool, I could picture Master Burbage but dimly. The only personage in London who stood out boldly in my mind —and that only by reputation—was the great Sir Walter Raleigh, the nearest of our absentee landlords in Cork.

Not that I expected help from Raleigh (even if he had known me from Adam's off-ox). That worthy gentleman, for all the riches granted him by the Queen when he had been her reigning lover, no longer enjoyed royal esteem. Her Majesty did not favor rivals on the field of love, even though her former partner had retired with honor. When the gallant Sir Walter had revealed his marriage to Lady Elizabeth Throckmorton (one of the Queen's own retinue), separate quarters at the Tower had been provided for both bride and groom. If I could believe the broadsides that found their way to Cork, the couple had been lucky to escape with their heads.

Raleigh had arranged their release after the Queen's rage had cooled—but Lady Raleigh had never dared to appear in court again. In Ireland we had chuckled over the story. Most of us approved of Raleigh; we savored the man's gallantry and dash. Besides, he had proved himself the least onerous of the various overlords the Queen had fastened on my unhappy homeland.

Most of his extensive land grants had been taken from those whose lives had been forfeit in the last savage rebellion against England, which had raged when I was a mere babe. It was this conflict that had first brought Raleigh to Ireland. Family legend had it that my mother had met him at this time —and that the dashing English captain had been her *grande passion*. True, she had mentioned him but seldom—and then, only to me. But I know that he had visited the Barry estate on the River Lee. These visits had occurred when the rebellion was only at the simmering stage. His purpose had been to seek out leaders among the gentry who would prove loyal to England when the time of troubles came. Naturally most of my country was ripe for revolt against the Protestantism to which the Queen gave at least tacit support. My mother's family, however, had always been Protestant—and Raleigh had made them his confidants.

Or so the story ran; as a youth, I had breathed in every word of it. It had seemed inevitable to me that my mother should be smitten by Raleigh's charm. Regardless of where he set foot in his heyday, the man had been a conquering hero, the jewel-and-velvet flower of what has been so justly called the English Renaissance. Even then he had charmed the Queen out of her interest in the Earl of Leicester, and was well on the way to becoming her reigning lover, a position he was to maintain for over a decade. What country maiden could resist a man of such fiery persuasion?

I will speculate no further on this matter. It is not for a dutiful son to say where tongue wagging left off and fact began. But I am positive that my mother's betrothal to MacManus had been arranged by my grandparents to remove her from the dashing English captain's orbit. And I am equally sure that a sigh of relief rose from the banks of the River Lee when their marriage was certified by my birth, exactly nine courses of the moon following the posting of the banns.

Perhaps I have implied more than I should in these hazy romancings. As I have said, nothing was farther from my hopes than a meeting with Raleigh, now that I was London-bound at last. Such plans as I had (when does a carefree youth of twenty-one need a map for the future when he goes adventuring?) were centered on the theater of Master Burbage—and the figure I hoped to cut there when I had forced an entrance.

The weather was fine when my ship deposited me at Liverpool, and my purse was none too heavy—so I decided to advance on the English metropolis afoot. I had not disdained a lift when one was offered; nor had I minded the poor roads or other hazards. Remember that I was an outlander (a colonial, if you will), with too much education and too little background. Remember, too, that these first glimpses of the England of my dreams were as thrilling as an unopened book, and just as mysterious. Who can blame me for lingering a little on the way?

Only yesterday I had strolled down the high street of Stratford, a village on the Avon, said to be the birthplace of one Will Shakespeare, a scrivener in Burbage's employ. When I turned the bend in the road that led to Oxford (the spires of the university were already in view) I was debating the wisdom of my last detour. Might it not have been wiser to push on to London before my money was gone?

It was then that I first glimpsed the stranded coach—and the dark enchantress who had stepped from the wreck and now stood in silhouette against the westering sun, like man's first temptation made visible.

I guessed her nationality instantly, even before my ear caught the shouted oaths of her companion. An odder pair would be hard to vision, but the man was more gnome than human, a thin-faced devil who must have been all of sixty. The fine satin doublet he was wearing, as well as his chains and rings, proclaimed a person of quality, though the imprecations he was shouting in Spanish (a language well suited to cursing) would not have disgraced the guard room. The privilege of easing one's choler in blasphemy, as I knew, was a court custom in England, enjoyed by ladies and gentlemen alike.

"Por los entrados, imbecile! Can you do nothing?"

The object of this diatribe was the coachman, a swarthy fellow who knelt on hands and knees in a vain effort to extract the broken spring. The girl seemed to enjoy the situation. At least she gave me a smile as I came abreast of the little group, and her lynx-green eyes opened wide to add to that saucy challenge. It was enough to sweep my hat from my head in as deep a bow as an Irishman can offer.

"May I help, señorita?" I asked, using her native tongue.

If my charmer was startled to hear good Spanish from a stranger, she gave no sign. "If you are a mender of coaches, señor," she said in a husky contralto that teased my senses no less than her cat-eyed boldness, "you are sent from heaven."

Our exchange had given the satin-clad gnome a chance to turn from the carriage. He fixed me with a piercing look I would remember later, a stare that was both resentful and incredulous.

"Who are you?"

Again I made my best leg: in the circumstances I could overlook his ogling, along with his poor manners. "The name is Shawn MacManus, sir," I said. "A traveler from Cork."

"An Irishman who speaks Spanish?"

"My father saw to my education, señor. May I inspect the damage?"

With my help the coachman was soon able to remove the broken spring. Together we hacked a stout sapling from the nearest copse: a length of rope from the box, I saw, would be sufficient to lash it into place beneath the carriage and raise that cumbersome weight from the wheels. I worked rapidly, aware that the don's eyes had never left my face. Clearly there was something about me that had stirred mischief in his brain, though he seemed hesitant to question me further.

I will confess that I made the most of the last, dramatic moment—stripping to the waist before I arched my back beneath the wheel. Girl and man were staring when I cracked my sinews in a supreme effort that lifted the coach clear of the roadbed and held it suspended while the driver eased the sapling into place and lashed it there. It was hardly the occasion to remark that I had won a dozen weight-lifting contests at the fairings. The amazement in the girl's eyes, when I rose from my labors as coolly as I had commenced them, was reward enough.

"That will take you into Oxford," I said. "Do you plan to rest there tonight?"

"We sleep at the Swan and Dolphin," said the don. "Perhaps you will join us at dinner—as a reward for your industry?" The man's tone was now silken-smooth. Somehow, I liked it less than his brusqueness.

"The service was nothing, señor——"

"I am Don Pedro de Quesada, Señor MacManus—assistant to the Spanish ambassador at the English court. This is my niece and ward, Doña Elvira Moreno y Quesada."

I bent to kiss the hand the girl offered me. Quesada was known through all of Protestant Britain as one of the cleverest agents of Spain. His master, King Philip, ever a tireless intriguer, was still a formidable foe, despite the blow he had suffered with the loss of his Armada. As his representative in London, Quesada's task was to discourage the court's sponsorship of forays against Spanish ports and shipping. A less persistent enemy than His Most Catholic Majesty would have long since broken off relations with the English Crown—but Philip, who grew no less bigoted with age, still hoped to bend that country to his will. Quesada (or so I had been informed) had made himself indispensable as a liaison between Madrid and the English Catholics, who still dreamed of overthrowing Elizabeth and restoring their religion as the official faith of Britain.

Of course none of this mattered one whit to Shawn MacManus, a dramatist in embryo, avid for the first caress of fortune. Quesada was in my debt—however slightly. If he had invited me to dine with a special motive, I resolved to exploit it to the full, whatever the source of his interest.

"You honor me too highly, Don Pedro," I said. "However, I'll accept your offer."

"*Saludable, señor*. Will you hand my niece into the coach?"

The comely Elvira, who had only just released my hand, laid her fingers on my arm again as I assisted her up the step—a maneuver that permitted me a tantalizing glimpse of her neatly turned ankles. Quesada had gone forward to give orders to his coachman, so I dared to spring in after her. My spirits soared when she took my hand of her own volition and gave it a prodigious squeeze.

"Are you always this direct?" she whispered.

"Why not—when the game's worth the candle?"

There was no time for more, since Don Pedro was already in the doorframe. On the drive to Oxford he talked constantly —though I will admit that I paid scant heed to his discourse —while his niece's hand continued to nest in mind. For the most part, it was a question-and-answer catechism, with myself as the subject. I responded good-humoredly, since it was flattering to have so fine a gentleman solicitous of my future —even though his motive still escaped me.

"Why did you leave Ireland, señor? With your father's help, you might easily have carved your niche there."

"Ireland holds no future for a dramatist," I said.

"You consider the writing of plays a proper calling?"

"I'm told it's a rewarding one in London," I said. "Once I've forced the door of the theater, I'll find ways to prove myself. Why shouldn't I make myself the equal of Robert Greene —or Will Shakespeare?"

Niece and uncle exchanged a glance—and Doña Elvira laughed softly. "Are you familiar with the plays of Master Shakespeare?"

"Only in folio," I admitted. "Judging them as a student, I cannot say I fear his competition."

"Don't tease the boy," said Don Pedro. "Proper self-respect's a precious attribute of youth." His tone was gentle enough, yet it was more command than suggestion. Evidently he had decided that my feelings must not be ruffled, even by such gentle raillery. For my part I would have preferred to discuss Will Shakespeare further. Naturally I had only been twitting the girl: I was well aware that his dramas were above my present powers to equal.

However, since it was her uncle's whim to quiz me, I offered no objection—while pressing against her pliant body as snugly as her stays would permit. So we remained, while King Philip's envoy rehearsed my past, including the date of my birth, which he was at some pains to establish.

" 'Tis a fine thing to be twenty in Elizabeth Tudor's England," he said finally. "Come to me if you have no luck with Burbage, and I'll put in a word for you."

At the inn in Oxford, Quesada was the grandee once again, scolding the waiters as he ordered our dinners, pooh-poohing the wine, and touring the ancient ordinary from top to bottom before he found chambers that pleased him. Over my protests he insisted on paying in advance for both my food and lodging.

"I've a real reason for keeping you nearby," he told me. "When we've dined, I must go to the university to consult with a learned friend at Balliol. I'd prefer to stay the night, since the matter we're discussing is a lengthy one. Frankly, Señor MacManus, I would be easier in my mind if my niece had a gentleman nearby to guard her."

Since these were precisely my own sentiments, I could do no less than agree to become his guest. All through the sumptuous dinner I searched for some flaw in his courtesy—and found none. When the wine had been passed for the third time (and I had taken another helping of the roast swan for which the inn was famous) I'd begun to wonder if I had misjudged him.

In Spain, I am told, women seldom appear at table with their men, but Elvira followed the English custom, seating herself at the foot of the groaning board and matching us bumper for bumper. Outwardly she remained demure enough, contenting herself with a sly wink or two when Don Pedro's eyes were elsewhere. When the wine waiter approached me for the last time, I will confess that I was mellow indeed—so filled with well-being, in fact, that I was prepared to take them both at their face value.

At the meal's close Doña Elvira again followed the English custom, withdrawing to her uncle's suite upstairs while Quesada and I cracked nuts before the fire and poured a last glass. As she withdrew she bade me good night with a lifted brow that spoke volumes. True to his resolve, Don Pedro departed almost at once. I waved him a farewell from the downstairs

window of the inn and continued to sit with the decanter before me while I fought a losing battle with my conscience.

When my conscience had won I rose at last and went up
the stair on tiptoe, that I might pass her door without a sound.
Once I was inside my own chamber, I bolted the door, kicked
off my boots, and cursed knight-errant MacManus thoroughly
while I fumbled in my rucksack for a nightshirt to clothe
MacManus the unregenerate libertine. It was then that the curtains on the four-poster stirred faintly. Even in the dance of
the candle end, there was no mistaking the head and shoulders
that were thrust out to greet me, or the white arm that beckoned me closer.

"Where have you been, *novio mío?*" asked Elvira. "I thought
you were never coming."

We had sported until dawn, when she fell asleep at last. As
I say, I was the first to waken. Now that I have told the story
fairly, is there any wonder at my puzzlement?

My black-haired temptress still slept, though the sun was
now well risen. Fully dressed and hesitating to waken her, I
unlocked the door quietly and slipped into the hall. Applying
my eye to the keyhole of the suite beyond, I was not too startled to observe Quesada—in a frogged dressing gown and already at breakfast. The nightcap that rode jauntily on his un-
combed white thatch was proof enough that his absence had
not been prolonged. By the same token, he must have known
just where his niece had passed the night.

When I returned to my own room Elvira did not seem disposed to waken, even when I bent to kiss her.

"You must go," I whispered, "before your uncle returns."

She opened her eyes then and stared up at me questioningly
before her mouth softened in a smile. *"Gracias, hombre,"* she
said, and arched her back in a yawn of pure content.

" 'Tis I who should thank you."

"Because I sought out your bed? When I saw you lift our
coach—as easily as I might lift a bandbox—I knew I must
have you or die." She chuckled then, deep in her throat; in
her half-closed eyes I caught a glint of the feline fire that had
stirred my pulses at our first meeting. The hands that framed
my face, as she lifted from the bed to embrace me, were gentle enough. Why did I have the illusion that I was between the
claws of a tigress?

"Soul of my heart," I said in Spanish, a language in which such compliments seem entirely natural, "it was an enchantment."

"A night to remember always," she agreed. "But you are right—it is also time to go."

Elvira had worn only a cloak when she entered my door. This morning, after she rose from the bed, she stood yawning in the bath of sunlight at the window—as though still reluctant to leave me. It was a pause that gave me ample opportunity to admire her charms before I folded the cloak around her nakedness. She went out with only a cursory glance to make sure the corridor was empty—and was back in a moment, smiling broadly.

"As I hoped, he passed the night in Oxford," she said. "Still, it might be wiser if you left now."

"He offered me a ride to London. How will you explain my absence?"

"I'll think of some excuse. Hurry, *chiquito*. The coach may drive up at any moment."

I lifted my rucksack. "When will I see you again?"

"I'm a virtual prisoner in London."

"Try to send me word at the Theatre——"

"We'll find ways," she said, and stood on tiptoe to kiss me before she led me into the shadowed hall.

At the bottom tread I listened until the door of the suite had sighed shut above. I was upstairs again in a trice, with an eye to the keyhole. Quesada, still at table, was in the act of spearing a bacon rasher. With his fork in mid-air, he grinned at the minx, who had curled up in the chair next to his and was whispering in his ear.

I heard their laughter, though I could not catch their words. Long before I took the highroad I was chuckling too —though I could not be sure whether I was laughing at Elvira Quesada or myself.

CHAPTER II

The Theatre in the Fields

LONDON, I told myself, could await my arrival another night. Once clear of Oxford, I left the highroad and took a more circuitous route lest Don Pedro's coach overtake me. Whatever the Spaniard's game might be, I knew he had no wish to encounter me in the near future. For my part I had resolved to keep clear of Elvira's enticements until I had established myself.

I spent that night in a farmer's haymow, deeming it prudent to conserve what remained in my purse. The following day, I made another circle, so as to approach the city by way of Finsbury Fields, which lay northeast of its walls. I had done this deliberately, that I might have the earliest possible view of Richard Burbage's Theatre, the first real structure of its kind in England. Long before I glimpsed it I saw that the playing flag was flying above its rooftree—a banner brave with blue stars and a golden lion rampant. My heart began to beat faster at the sight, a sure advertisement of the fact that actors would be treading its boards in a few hours' time.

Like the maps and books on London that I had read in Ireland, the Theatre (it had no other name) had been the object of my study for many years. When I made the last turning and stood within clear view, I found the actual edifice a trifle disappointing. I had pictured a rounded fortress of the arts, whose steep-pitched roofs all but touched the skies. Actually the Theatre was on the squat side, a building with the air of a dandy who refused to show his age. It was bright with playbills in all states of disrepair, and slapped with fresh whitewash to its straw-thatch eaves. Hawkers' booths clustered at its flanks; like the ticket windows, they were still closed at this early hour, though I knew that long queues would soon be forming to purchase standing space in the pit.

Three times I circled the playhouse before I dared to enter it. The approach I chose was a muddy alley at the rear, which gave in turn to a stout oaken door that stood a trifle ajar—enough, at any rate, to permit me to wriggle through. I found myself in a second passage, which led past a carpenter's shop to the apron of the stage. Here a set of steps descended to the open central portion, or pit. Once I had gained this well-trampled paradise of the groundlings (as the standing spectators were called), I could understand the structure of the Theatre, and its purpose.

At first glance it reminded me of our bear-baiting pit in Cork—a circular amphitheater open to the sky, the tiered seats that surrounded it protected by a thatched roof. The stage itself, embraced in the double curve of these balconies, was covered by an extension of this same rough thatch, save for the flaring outer portion, or apron. Thus, both performers and seat holders were shielded from rainstorms; only the groundlings were exposed to the elements—and these hardy fellows were used to inclement weather, since they had always stood in the tavern yards, the only playhouses most Englishmen had ever known.

So far, no one had challenged my right to explore. I found the stair leading to the first balcony level, and chose one of the curving tiers of seats that hung so precariously above the stage. Behind the jutting apron I now observed a smaller acting area, masked by curtains; this, I knew, was used for special scenic effects, such as a cave or bedroom. The curtains were seldom opened. Most of the plays in the Theatre's repertory were of the sort that needed ample stage room for ranting. Besides, such was the clergy's hatred of the drama, it was considered unwise to offer so intimate a scene as a bedroom, even if its occupants were married.

It was because of this bitter-end opposition to drama in all its forms that James Burbage (the father of Richard the actor) had built his Theatre outside the walls of London. The location, near Bishopsgate, was known as Shoreditch, and lay beyond the jurisdiction of the city council. The liberties that the present actor-manager enjoyed here had been granted by the Queen herself. Her Majesty's love for the play was well known. Here in Shoreditch, Dick Burbage was safe from the harassments and the censorship of London's stiff-necked city government, whose holier-than-thou delegates always had a Puritan majority.

Musing on these matters, I was unaware that I no longer had the Theatre to myself, until I heard the creak of a loose floor board below. A slender lad had just strolled on stage from the curtained inner section—a youth with clubbed red curls and a mincing gait that could only be described as effeminate. His trunk hose revealed rounded limbs that were definitely girlish in character. I grinned to myself, proud that I was already worldling enough to recognize one of the boy apprentices. When this lad began to declaim a few lines (cautiously, at first, then with rising volume, until the high but pleasingly feminine voice seemed to fill the Theatre) the picture was complete.

I soon found myself enraptured by the passage he was reciting, which I recognized as a soliloquy from the *Faustus* of Marlowe.

> *Oh, what a world of profit and delight,*
> *Of power, of honour and omnipotence*
> *Is promised to the studious artisan!*
> *All things that move between the quiet poles*
> *Shall be at my command. Emperors and kings*
> *Are but obeyed in their several provinces—*
> *Nor can they raise the wind or rend the clouds—*
> *But his dominion—that exceeds in this*
> *Stretches as far as doth the mind of man.*

At the finish of the declamation I could not resist the impulse to applaud. The lad paused as abruptly as a forest fawn and seemed about to flee the stage. Then, squaring frail shoulders, he strode to the edge of the apron and looked upward until he could spy me out in the first tier of seats. At that closer view, I was even more startled than the actor—for what I had considered a boy was, in truth, a shapely young woman.

I had already noted the rounded perfection of her limbs. Now, in the bath of sunlight that spilled across the apron, I could detect the swelling fullness of young breasts beneath her tunic. A moment before (when I was unaware of her sex), I had felt no sense of guilt as I spied on her soliloquy. Con-

fused by the discovery I had made, I could only consider myself an eavesdropper—and spoke up quickly, to conquer the
lump in my throat.

"Bravo, mistress!" I shouted. "Well spoken indeed."

"What are you doing here?" the lass demanded. (I could
see that she was no more than that, despite her tone of hostile
authority.)

"No one denied me entrance."

"You'll not avoid paying your fee by sneaking in."

With a little gold still in my pocket, I could ignore that rasp
to my feelings—though I felt I must reply in kind. "Hold
your tongue, my young filly," I shouted back. "Impugn my
honesty and I'll say you screeched like a crow."

The girl, I saw, had a temper that blazed quickly. Snatching
up a quarterstaff that leaned against the apron, she balanced it
on her palm like a javelin, saw it would be a far toss indeed
across the pit, and shook a fist at me instead. "Come down
here and say that, you black-maned dog," she cried. "Unless
you're afraid of a mere girl."

"An Irishman fears no man alive," I replied. With each
word I was enjoying this game of insults more. To prove it, I
anchored both hands on the balcony rail and swung to ground
level. "Why should I fear a lass?" I ducked in time, as the
quarterstaff just missed my ear. "Not even a lass who shows
her limbs in hose."

She had the grace to blush at that—or perhaps it was only
chagrin because the quarterstaff had missed its target. In any
event she stood her ground—and her chin lifted proudly as I
reached the apron in a single leap.

"What's wrong with my legs, pray?"

"Now that I can see them better, nothing."

A less forthright maid would have scurried to cover at my
admiring scrutiny. This one, as I had expected, took refuge
again in temper. "By what right d'you play Peeping Thomas
in the best-priced seats?" she demanded. "The Theatre is not
even open yet."

"Then why are you here?"

"I *live* here. My father is the chief stage keeper."

"Are you his assistant?"

"That I am, master." Already I could feel that her anger at
my intrusion was ebbing—that she realized my interest was
genuine.

"How are you called?"

"My name is Susanna Field—and I have already spoken lines on this stage. Why should boys take the women's parts when we could do them better?"

"From what I've seen, you speak truth," I said.

"So now you're a judge of acting, as well as an interloper. What's your name and business?"

"The name is Shawn MacManus—and, like you, I seek a career in this theater."

"A rebel Irishman—I expected as much."

"A *loyal* Irishman. Loyal to the Queen, and a good Protestant."

She just escaped returning my grin. "At least you're no Puritan, Master McManus—else you'd be preaching me a sermon on my attire."

" 'Tis you who are the Puritan, with the name Susanna."

The girl dropped her eyes. "My mother named me," she said. "She never approved my father's work. The plague took her while I was still a child—so I've only the name to show for a proper upbringing."

"Someone bequeathed you a peckish tongue as well," I observed. "Or should I say *a tiger's heart, wrapped in a player's hide?*"

Her eyes opened wide at that. "You've read the plays of Robert Greene?"

"Enough to quote from them. I'd hoped to study under him."

"Master Robert died a year ago. All of us mourned his passing—all, that is, but Will Shakespeare. The line you just spoke brings their quarrels to mind. You've heard of him, no doubt."

"Of course," I said, pleased that she was permitting me to talk as an equal.

Susanna took a stance, an action that thrust her young bosom forward in a most teasing fashion. *"There is an upstart crow,"* she declaimed, *"beautified with feathers that, with his tiger's heart wrapped in a player's hide, supposes he is as well able to bombast out a blank verse as the best of you. And, being an absolute Johannes Factotem, is, in his own conceit, the only shakescene in the country!"*

While she intoned this bombast the girl strutted about the stage in such a convincing caricature of a pouter pigeon that I (finding myself an audience of one again) burst out laughing. "I'd like to see this Master Shakescene in the flesh," I said.

She came out of her posturing: in a flash she was sparring with me for her own amusement—and unsure, even now, whether to take me seriously. "The truth is, I've maligned our Will," she said. "Perhaps you should meet him and judge for yourself. If I present you, will you stop playing the barbarian?"

"Give me the chance," I said. "I'll prove I was born a gentleman."

Susanna circled me slowly, the better to judge me from every angle. "Your countrymen speak as fancy moves them," she said. "Do you really wish to make the theater your career?"

"It's the one thing I've wanted," I told her earnestly.

She looked into my eyes then and seemed to like what she found there. "Why should a man in his right mind choose playwriting as his life work?"

"Have you asked Master Will that question?"

"That I've not," said Susanna, with a toss of her head. "Nor would I advise you to make so bold. Master Shakescene likes to consider himself a poet as well as a dramatist. Would you call yourself a poet too?"

"Why not—with a teacher like you to inspire me?"

She colored at my bearlike compliment—and I was sure that my hypnotic power with the weaker sex (a magnetism I mention with no false modesty, since it often functioned despite my own best resolves) had won me yet another prize. The conviction deepened when I took her hand and she made no effort to withdraw it.

"Let me prove myself," I said. "You've already promised as much."

A deep voice, booming from the murky regions behind the inner curtain, cut through my plea before I could press my advantage further. It was an actor's voice in the manner born, as real as off-stage thunder.

"Are you prancing on stage, Puss?"

"Yes, Master Richard," the girl called back.

"Come to the sewing room. I've a gorget that needs mending."

I had dropped Susanna's hand at the interruption. Now, as

our eyes met again, she seemed to make up her mind and linked firm fingers with mine.

"Follow me, Master Shawn," she whispered. "I'll be your guide backstage. 'Tis a gloomy place for a newcomer."

"Where are you taking me?"

"To meet Dick Burbage—where else? He owns this theater with his brother, Master Cuthbert."

The area behind the draw curtains, as Susanna had warned me, was black indeed, but the girl moved among the looming set pieces that served as scenery with the confidence of a homing sparrow. In another moment we stood in the sewing room, which, as I was to learn later, was her special domain. A half dozen apprentices labored busily at the workbenches along the wall, plying their bodkins with a kind of desperate urgency as though Beelzebub was waiting to snatch the tardiest. Here and there, lips moved above the flashing needles as small-part actors (who doubled in brass, as it were) rehearsed their lines.

At another time I would have taken in such details with avid interest. Today the voices reached me but dimly, bedazzled as I was at this chance to meet England's finest actor. My audacity, it seemed, had served me on the bare boards of the Theatre, no less unexpectedly than the four-poster at the Swan and Dolphin. So great, in fact, was my exuberance that I could not quite keep down a gasp when I found myself face to face with the object of my long journey.

Master Richard Burbage stood before a dusty window frame which cast a nimbus about his straw-blond head. He was slender and of medium height. (This was a fact I verified later. At the time he seemed tall as some god from Olympus.) Each of his motions was a thing of grace, albeit on the studied side. The fact that he was naked to the waist and carried a torn doublet on one arm did not detract from his poise. His face was set in a mocking smile—but who can picture the face of a mime, when it but served as a mirror for all the passions known to man?

"We've come to expect stray cats from you, Susanna," he said, with a great booming laugh. "But this is something different. What is it?"

Despite the words, I could sense that he had no real wish to wound me. Some of my awe deserted me as I returned his grin. "Call me a visitor whose eagerness has exceeded his decorum, sir," I said.

"The name," Susanna added, "is Shawn MacManus. He claims to be a loyal Irishman."

Burbage's eyebrows climbed still higher. "The Queen will be glad to learn there's at least one of you," he said. "What can we do for you here, young master?"

I forced myself to speak boldly. "Already I'm by way of being a writer of verses for masques and mummers," I said. "I've come to England to sharpen my gifts."

"So have half the varlets in London," he said.

"I've planned this visit for years, sir. If you'd let me work here, I'd be forever in your debt."

The eyebrows, which had arched in laughter, now knitted in a scowl so intense that I needed all my courage to stand my ground. Even then, part of my brain recognized the oldest of attacks in the performer's arsenal, the swift change of mood. "Is that rucksack heavy with unread masterworks?"

"I tore up my juvenilia when I set sail for England," I said. "I'm here only to learn."

"As a writer of plays? My theater bursts with playwrights. At this moment it's a seasick bark that rocks with their wind. Would you add to the afflatus, Master Shawn?"

"Not until I'm ready. Meanwhile I'll sweep your stage if need be. I'll even ply a needle for Mistress Susanna—or outbox your groundlings if they threaten to howl down a performance."

"Why here? There are other playhouses. Try the Swan—or the Rose."

"When a man seeks enlightenment, he goes to the source," I said. "This is the only theater in England that needs no second label."

Burbage growled in his throat, then circled me slowly—much as Susanna had done. "You're either sincere or you've an uncommon glib tongue," he said. "And I'll grant you're a fine figure of a man. Unfortunately we've no need at present for more muscle."

Susanna, who had perched on an empty bench, spoke up with the spryness I had already found so pleasing. "Is Ned Blake over the quinsy?"

"He is not, Puss, as you well know," said Burbage testily.

"One of us must speak his part again today. Are you begging off as Joan, so you may act as Ned's substitute?"

The girl's eyes flashed: when she stood eye to eye with Burbage I saw they were of a height. While he had ranted at me he had seemed at least a yard taller.

"You promised I could play Joan," she all but screeched. "Would you go back on your word?"

"Not if you're headstrong enough to risk it," he said. "Are you suggesting we give Ned's place to this outlander?"

"Why not?"

"Tell me first how brave *you'll* be at the starting trumpet, my girl," he said. "I'm risking enough on you. Why should I risk more?"

"I can speak any part. I've already proved I could play Joan at the rehearsal."

"A rehearsal's one thing, Puss, an audience another. What if they rip out my seats and belabor the actors? It's happened before."

"*Henry VI* has already succeeded here. It'll succeed this afternoon as well."

Burbage had not quite done with his inspection. "You're already half dressed for the part, I see." His thumb and forefinger darted forward to tweak one of the breasts beneath the girl's thin shirt. "How will you disguise those nubbins, lass? They'll betray you fast enough."

Susanna did not flinch under his touch. "I'll wear a loose tunic," she said. "And a tight binding. Besides, this part calls for a girl in boy's clothing."

"So it does. Have you permission from your father?"

"I'll handle him, never fear."

"And now you propose to handle me—until I give this young brute a chance?"

"Ned's part calls for a brute," said the girl, as calmly as though I were not present. "I can teach him the lines in an hour."

"So you can, my dear—you've an uncommon gift for planting words in empty skulls." He gave up his circling and assumed a pedagogue's stance, with a fist knotted at his back and a finger to his nose. When he turned to level the finger at my midriff I knew that Susanna had won.

"What say you, boy?"

"I'll try anything once, sir."

He tossed his doublet into my arms. "As Susanna's told you, the part calls for only a line or so and a great dog in uniform—so it's likely you'll do."

"I can't thank you enough——"

"Don't thank me yet; you're not hired unless that doublet's as good as new before our performance. You see, Master Shawn, I've more ways than one of testing you."

"The doublet will be ready," I promised. "So will my lines."

"Set to, then, lad—and do what Susanna orders. You'll find her a hard taskmaster. Any more questions—including wages?"

"That's for you to set, master."

"I'll give you a penny a day, so long as Ned is sick. Providing, of course, you aren't hooted off the stage."

He left us on that, with his booming laugh. I stared after his exit with my mouth agape—unable to credit my luck even now. Susanna's sharp elbow roused me from my reverie quickly enough.

"Can you really ply a bodkin, Shawn MacManus? Or was that another of your fibs?"

"Fetch me a needle," I said. "And give me my lines while I work. I'll prove I can stitch as neatly as any housewife."

CHAPTER III

Master Will

BURBAGE HAD spoken truly when he described Susanna as a hard taskmaster. In the next hour (while I bustled at her heels in the sewing and property rooms) she drilled the lines of my short part into my head so firmly that there was no chance of forgetting them.

As the time of our performance approached—and other, more important actors began to drift through the stage alley, singly or in groups—the tempo of Susanna's activities increased. I had already gathered that in addition to her duties as seamstress she worked with her father as a prompter, and had long since committed most of the plays to memory. In addition to that task, she was a girl-of-all-work in the clut-

tered backstage area. Here she was not above repairing a rent
in an actor's costume in the last moment before his entrance,
or helping to lash down the ponderous bits of scenery that
seemed ready to fall apart at the slightest breath.

Helping when I could, watching the comings and goings of
countless folk behind the inner curtain (many of who seemed
interlopers with a whole bazaar of unlikely commodities to
sell), I was sure the scene was Bedlam at its worst. And yet,
even in my ignorance, I sensed an underlying pattern which
imposed itself by degrees in the last half hour before the
opening of the current playbill. Little by little, the hangers-on
were banished, the sellers of baubles driven to their lairs outside the Theatre walls. At last even Susanna ceased her bustling and led me to the spot where I would await my entrance
cue.

"Don't speak until Jaimie signals," she said. "Above all,
don't forget that you're now part of the performance though
you've only fifty words. I'm letting you stand where you can
watch—as a special reward."

Jamie gave me a harried signal to let me know he had
overheard. The stage keeper at the Theatre was a bulky fellow
who resembled nothing so much as a disorderly sheep dog
with a far larger flock than he could manage. But I saw he
was in command here, despite his air of breathless bustle—
and the quick hug he bestowed upon his daughter before he
scurried across the stage was insurance enough of his affection.
Their slightly cavalier manner toward each other, and the
fact that Susanna called her father by his Christian name,
seemed only natural in this bizarre spot.

My uniform (I was impersonating a captain of the guard in
the closing scene) had needed a great deal of ripping and
splicing before it would fit my massive frame. Susanna had
quite literally stitched me into it—so that I was forced to hold
my breath lest I pop at every gusset. For her part, she had
bound herself—to preserve the illusion that a boy was reading
the part of Joan—so tightly that we resembled a pair of
trussed fowls.

Susanna had given me the outline of today's play in bits
and snatches while she attended to more pressing matters.
Written by Master Shakespeare himself, it dealt with the Wars
of the Roses, and seemed a blood-drenched affair, though I

had but a dim notion of the story beyond my own small contribution.

While our preparations continued I could hear the groundlings pour in, a roar of voices that shook the inner curtain. The standing space, which sold for a penny, was always at a premium, and the pit was usually jammed long before a performance. The tiered seats were slower in filling; these were priced as high as a shilling, as were the stools in the corners of the stage itself, where it was customary for the gallants to display their finery—and, on occasion, to trade witticisms with the actors.

From the glances I stole at the peephole, I realized that today's bill had drawn a goodly audience. Except for the noise, the crowd seemed orderly enough so far. It was only in the wings, as the company assembled for their various entrances, that quarrels flared. Only Burbage (in a quilted dressing sack that hid his splendid costume) seemed to grow calmer as the great moment approached. It was as though he drew sustenance from the air about him—the same air I now found it difficult to breathe, for reasons which had little to do with the tightness of my tunic.

Finally a trumpet sounded three times outside the playhouse walls—a summons for the drinkers to leave the refreshment booths and the orange vendors to quit the galleries. There was a short wait while the last of the gallants scampered on stage to quarrel good-naturedly for the remaining stools. . . . The heralds were already in their places on the apron. As their trumpets blared, a cloud of pigeons rose from the rooftree, then fluttered back, as though they, too, wished to witness the play's first scene.

Because of my vantage point just inside the curtain, I could see all that transpired without revealing myself to the groundlings. Since most of the performers made their entrances from my side, I could also observe the metamorphosis that changed a clown in armor to a thing of flesh and blood the moment these strange, puppetlike creatures stalked out to join the drama that was building before my enraptured eyes.

My knowledge of the Wars of the Roses was slight enough; I knew even less of Henry VI, the monarch who took so large a part in those bitter struggles. But I could feel myself a witness of history in the making long before Lord Talbot's first entrance—and I could sense, from the deep silence beyond the apron (to say nothing of the frequent thunders of applause), that the audience was sharing my feelings. Did it matter that Master Shakespeare was not above twisting that same history to his own ends, so long as the story he unfolded held us all in a grip of iron?

Susanna had told me the dramatist himself would be reading Talbot's part this afternoon, so I was prepared for his appearance in the wings. Master Will was not, at first view, an imposing figure. He was almost dumpy in his armor—and, since he still carried his casque on one arm, he seemed shrunken, like a turtle emerging from its shell. But the face he thrust up at mine was an arresting one—long and mobile, with a strong chin under the lazy-man's beard and burning brown eyes that seemed to pin me to the wall.

"Are you the fellow who's speaking Ned Blake's lines?"

"I am, sir."

"See that you speak them well. My Lord Essex is in the audience."

"The lover of the Queen—I mean her favorite?"

"Your first try was the better," said Shakespeare dryly. "If Essex likes my play, we'll have the whole court to see it."

"I'll do my best, sir."

"See that you remember then," he said in the same waspish whisper, adjusting his sword so it could be readily drawn. Then, taking his entrance cue, he strode into the swirling action on stage.

The scene that followed was a high point in this story of royal misadventures and a fine example for a would-be dramatist to study. Whatever the abilities of Master Will as an actor (he seemed, at times, a trifle shrill to my ear), he was a past master of dialogue. The lines sang, lifting the actors with them, speeding the play to its first climax—then on to another, as the action mounted. By now the audience was spellbound; from my own vantage point I was just as mesmerized by the skill and grace of the company as when they fought with blazing words—or, on occasion, with bare swords, so fiercely that I was half persuaded the battle was real.

Susanna was playing the part of Joan of Arc, the crafty French peasant maid who hoodwinked our armies with the assistance of devils and thus defeated us time and again on the field of battle. As the girl played her, this Joan was a lusty lass. Though she was a mortal enemy of the English, I could not help admiring Susanna's skill. (Once, when she appeared suddenly on a turret with an outthrust torch, I held my breath, positive she must tumble to her death.) Throughout, I am sure, no one suspected that a girl was playing the part—at least there was no leering, not even from the gallants who were near enough to touch her.

My own entrance occurred when Lord Talbot, in the person of Master Shakespeare, lay dying. James Field, I had observed, was adept at shoving lesser actors into the melee as their presence was required. As I had expected, my own shove came in time. I found myself standing on the stage of the Theatre at last, with the sun dazzling my eyeballs, awaiting my cue to declaim.

I had only a confused impression of thronging faces, as groundlings and gallants leaned forward with the same rapt attention. Apparently no one had noticed me, a fact which piqued me slightly until I realized that Master Will, as was his right, was the cynosure of every eye while he gasped out Lord Talbot's final lines and collapsed in death. Even then, the attention of the audience remained fixed on the corpse—as though it was hoping (by one of those miracles so commonplace in the drama) the noble lord might be made whole again before their eyes.

The scene had engrossed me too—so completely that I felt my vision blur with tears I made no attempt to restrain, since I could hear sobbing from the audience. It was a long time (by dramatic standards) before I heard the voice of Susanna's father in the wings, whispering a sentence that seemed familiar, then repeating the whisper with greater emphasis. Then (though his body was sprawled in simulated death) I caught the baleful glare of Will Shakespeare's eyes. The next instant I felt a stab at my backside, as the cause of the strained silence in the Theatre was suddenly apparent.

My own speech was overdue—and Jaimie Field had thrown me my cue in vain, "winging" it from off stage in a whisper meant for my ears alone. The words I should have spoken were a mere stage device to draw attention from the dead lord while the action of the play moved on. It was Richard Burbage himself who had pricked my buttocks with his sword, a sovereign means of transforming me from audience to actor.

With my rear still smarting, I found my tongue at last and

declaimed my fifty words—so loudly that the whole playhouse turned in my direction. Until I finished speaking I was undeniably the focal point of Master Will's drama. Then Burbage strode on stage and my brief moment of glory was over.

I held my place at the entrance while four assistant stage keepers, in the uniforms of English soldiers, made their solemn exit with the body of Lord Talbot on their shoulders. As he passed, Master Shakespeare managed to swivel his head enough to give me another murderous glare. Clearly I was in for it when the performance ended: if I clung to my place in the wings, it was not only to enjoy the conclusion of the play but to avoid the playwright.

The drama ended at last, to prolonged cheers. I joined in the melee backstage in the hope that I might somehow remain anonymous. Susanna, flushed with her exertions, was receiving compliments on every hand. Her portrayal of the bewitched maid had been a brilliant one, and I was sure that no mincing boy could have done it half so well. I was on my way to congratulate her in turn, when a voice I recognized all too well stopped me dead.

"Where's the idiot who played the captain of the guard?" It was Master Will, right enough, shouldering actors aside in his furious eagerness to find me. I fancy myself a man of courage —but this was a time when I would have flown the field could I have found a handy exit. I dared not turn tail and run, lest I burst my seams and leave the Theatre naked as a jay. Nor could I reach the sewing room (and the closet where my own garb awaited me), since the playwright now stood athwart the threshold, with his beard lifting like the quills of a porcupine. Cornered as I was, I squared my shoulders and approached with what coolness I could muster.

"You called, master?"

"Dolt! With but a dozen lines, must you forget them today of all days?"

"I remembered them, sir. But I was so held by your performance I forgot to speak."

I had said the words impulsively, yet they were true enough —and he understood I meant them. Actors are vain to the last man, since their very nature feeds on praise—and Master Will was no exception. Rage seemed to leave him, as the wind leaves a broken bellows, though he continued to study me with smoldering eyes.

"Whoever told you to become an actor did you a false turn," he said. "With those muscles, you'd do better to seek work as a porter."

Burbage stepped between us, and his voice was gentle. "Don't belabor the boy, Will," he said. "It was his first time on the boards."

"Thank you for the sword prick, sir," I managed.

"You'll have a sore tail for a while, lad: I'm afraid I thrust harder than need be."

" 'Twas no more than I deserved," I said. "The words came right afterward."

"And loudly enough to be heard at Bishopsgate." The playwright, it seemed, had recovered his choler. "Essex was moved by my death scene. I watched him as I lay there, and I saw tears in his eyes. Then this black Irishman must needs bellow his lines—naturally he shocked Essex out of his wits. Never have I seen Milord look so pale. If you've spoiled my chance to play for the Queen, Master Idiot, I'll see to it that you never act in London."

"I've no ambition to act," I said. "Only to write plays like yourself."

"A writer of plays—*you?*" But he said no more: instead, I saw his eyes widen, and followed his gaze to the lackey who had just entered from the stage alley. The man's livery was brilliant as a sunrise, with noble quarterings. I am a fair student of heraldry enough, at any rate, to understand the silence that had fallen on the backstage area.

Jaimie Field had already bustled up to question the visitor. "What d'you seek, my friend?"

"My master sends a message to one of you." The lackey was scowling at each of us in turn. Evidently he had delivered such tidings before and had small love of actors.

"Is it for Master Shakespeare?"

"We do not know his name. He is the captain of the guard. who spoke just after Lord Talbot died on the battlefield." The fellow's eye, roving from face to face, had fixed on mine at last. *"You're* the captain," he said. "The Earl of Essex sends his compliments—and invites you to sup with him at the tavern across the fields."

Though I could not quite believe my ears, I kept the astonishment from my face. Drawing myself to my full height, ignoring the ominous bursting of a dozen seams, I answered calmly.

"Give me a moment to change my dress, and I'll be with you," I said. With a cool glance at the shocked face of Will Shakespeare, I turned on my heel and strode toward the room where Susanna had put my clothes.

CHAPTER IV

Two Against One

THE THEATRE stood near Shoreditch Road, a direct route by coach from the Queen's palace at Whitehall and the riverside residences of the nobility. It was a longish drive—and a still longer walk for those who elected to arrive on shank's mare from the soot-red city to the south. Therefore it was customary for playgoers to take a stirrup cup and a joint of mutton before their return to the metropolis, and several raffish inns catering to these appetites had sprung up nearby. It was toward such an establishment that my guide conducted me in the last half hour of twilight.

I was but dimly conscious of London Town, a monstrous shadow that seemed to blot half the horizon as the night advanced, but, ignorant though I was, I sensed that the folk about me were city men in their best and worst. I held aloof from their trampling, laughing presence, still feeling very much the outlander—and still mightily puzzled by the summons that had rescued me from Will Shakespeare's wrath.

Not that I attempted to question the lackey while he led me toward the stairway of the inn, through a common room teeming with actors and spectators and thick with smoke and superlatives as the tosspots at the long trestle tables praised or damned the play according to their mood. Here and there, I noticed, people turned to stare at me—but I did not take their interest amiss. After all, I was now an actor. If I preened myself a bit as I mounted the stair, it was only because the attitude was expected of one who wore the buskin.

At a door upstairs my guide paused to knock. A parade-ground bellow bade us enter. Two men sat at table within, be-

fore a brisk fire. One (he was much the older) wore the garb
of a soldier; the other was dressed in the height of fashion,
with great puffed sleeves and a ruff on which his too handsome, petulant face seemed to ride like a boar's head on a
platter. When the lackey bowed to this magnificence I knew
he could be no less than Robert Devereux, the second Earl of
Essex and the most powerful man in England.

The Queen's lover favored me with a flick of the fingers
and seemed waiting for me to speak—but I could not leave
off staring so easily. With the firelight behind me, he seemed
less than thirty. If I reckoned truly, this would make Elizabeth Tudor old enough to be his grandame. It was no secret
that the Queen had only sharpened her lusts with the loss of
her youth—and Essex was said to be a studhorse second to
none.

"Your servant, milords," I managed at last, giving them my
best reverence.

"Make me no curtsies, fellow," said the older man. "I'm Sir
Roger Williams, a plain soldier. Come forward and we'll have
a look at you."

So far I had hardly received the expected tribute to my acting. But I felt I must walk warily—and so, advanced to the
full glow of the hearth. Essex gave me no more than a glance,
but the soldier blew air through both nostrils like a rutting
bull.

"By all the gods in Christendom," said Sir Roger. "It's as I
told you at the play. Can't you see he's Wat's spit and
image?"

"I'm far too young to judge," said Essex.

"Will you take my word?"

"Of course, Roger."

"He's Wat, fifteen years younger. And he had her in his
hand then—remember?"

"All too well," said Essex.

I saw that they had forgotten me entirely. "If Your Lord-
ship has finished his inspection—?"

Sir Roger cut in, kindly enough, as he summoned the lackey. "Bring a stool for the actor," he said, and poured me a
glass of wine. "To your health, Master MacManus." Later I
would ask myself how he had found out my name so quickly.
Now I was glad for the respite, since it gave me a chance to
study him in detail.

Roger Williams was a soldier of the old school and a genuine hero in his own right. He had taught Essex all he knew of war (if I could believe the broadsides, that knowledge was slim enough). So far he had served Milord both as a tutor and a father. The collaboration had borne its sinister fruit: Essex —for all his foppish ways—had direct access to the royal closet. Who was I to deny that he held England in his palm?

I came back from my musings when I felt his eyes upon me. Never before had I been studied with such open intensity, not even by Quesada or Master Shakespeare. To call Milord cruel would understate the case; the leisurely scrutiny was too casual for that. Why, I do not know, but I had, for an instant, the prickly sensation of facing some great beast. The long, sensitive fingers that stroked the jet-black beard only added to the illusion.

I lost my fear when he addressed me in a tone that was both kindly and indulgent. "Tell me, lad—d'you know Sir Walter Raleigh?"

I was taken aback by the question. "Only by reputation, sir. But he was a friend of my mother's years ago."

Sir Roger leaned forward. "How many years ago?"

"I don't know rightly, sir. It was before she married my father."

"Were you the first issue of that marriage?"

"I was."

"How old are you now?"

"Just twenty-one, sir."

The war horse nodded; I could have sworn that he exchanged a wink with Essex.

"That explains it, clearly enough," he said. "Our man was there at the time, seeking to wean Desmond from the rebellion."

The aside conveyed nothing to me, save for the reference to Desmond—a noble family that had sparked the revolt of the Irish Catholics.

"How came you to be an actor, Master Shawn?" asked Milord.

"That I'm not, sir. I'm in London to seek a career as a dramatist: it was only by chance that I took a small part today."

"You took it loudly enough," said Sir Roger.

"Burbage had just pricked me with his sword. I was so

taken by Lord Talbot's dying speech that I quite forgot my lines."

"That I can understand," said Essex grandly. "To die in battle as Lord Talbot did is the greatest glory man can achieve."

Shakespeare had said there were tears in Milord's eyes as he watched the death scene. Like so many men who have risen too rapidly, Essex was evidently tranced by his own legend; today (however briefly) he had simply identified himself with the expiring hero on stage. Sir Roger, who was made of different stuff, only guffawed at his protégé's pose.

"There's little enough of glory in battle," he said, "unless it's cutting a Spaniard's throat. D'you plan to stay on at the Theatre, my boy?"

"As long as they'll have me. Which won't be forever if Master Shakespeare's choler endures."

Essex smiled. "I know Will's temper of old," he said. "Tell me what stirred up this one."

"He hoped for your approval of the play," I explained. "A word from you, he vowed, would send the court flocking to see it. Now he's sure I've offended you."

Essex continued to rumble with laughter, but I could see that my words had pleased his vanity. "Tell Master Will that I was much moved by his performance," he said. "I shall certainly recommend *The History of Henry VI* to Her Majesty."

"You are most kind, sir," I murmured. "This will help me keep my foothold."

Again Essex and Sir Roger exchanged a nod. "Master Shakespeare will be glad to have your news," said the former. "Why don't you convey it?"

I got to my feet at once. "That I will, sir, if you'll excuse me——"

Essex's eyes were twinkling. "Obviously you're a novice at acting," he said. "Else you'd have thought to ask me for a purse."

"But, milord——"

"Never mind, you shall have it just the same. Sir Roger will fetch one."

My hosts exchanged yet another double nod. While Sir Roger was out of the chamber—a space of ten minutes or more—my lord continued to ply me with sack and exerted himself to be charming. By the time the old soldier returned with the purse, my head was swimming—partly from the wine, and also from the excitement of being treated as an equal by the Queen's favorite. Whatever his reason, I knew that Essex could make my fortune overnight, as he had done for others. In actual fact, such had been the case in his own meteoric rise. As we drank, I found myself recalling some of the stories I had heard.

Robert Devereux had lost his father at an early age, but even then he had been a child of considerable precocity. He had lived for a while with the family of Lord Burghley. His playmate in that household had been Robert Cecil, now a strong political rival. Graduating with honors from Cambridge University, he had enjoyed the life of a scholar until he was seventeen. At that age, he had been introduced at court by the Earl of Leicester, the Queen's lover and favorite for many years. From that point, it was hard to separate truth from scandal; perhaps both were really the same.

Leicester, it was said, had brought the dark-haired Adonis to Whitehall in the hope of centering the Queen's somewhat capricious affections on a target he could trust. In this he had a double purpose, for he wished to divert Elizabeth's interest from another courtier who was fast eclipsing him in her favor. The rival was none other than Raleigh. If I could believe the gossips, the Queen did not take to the newcomer—opening her boudoir to Sir Walter instead.

Some nine years ago Leicester had given young Devereux the command of a troop of English forces in France. Here the youth had shown a flair for war—outwitting the enemy by dash and speed and a willingness to risk the lives of his command. His victories had made him the darling of the masses. Knighted in the field, he had returned as the first gentleman of England. The key to the Queen's closet still needed winning—yet even before Raleigh's marriage the rise of Essex had been as swift as his rival's decline.

Now that he was in firm possession of the royal bed, his only real opponent was Lord Cecil, the playmate of his boyhood. On surface, the two posed as friends; beneath, it was war to the death—as Essex used his romantic power over the aging Elizabeth while Cecil relied on his position as the court's most trusted adviser in matters of state, to say nothing of his genius for satisfying his sovereign's love of gold.

These thoughts continued to run through my head while I

matched Milord drink for drink and jest for jest. Somehow, I told myself, a way must be found to turn this meeting to my own account—but I had yet to hit on it when Sir Roger returned with my purse. As he put it into my hand, I felt that it was a heavy one.

"You may take your leave, lad," he said. "Our Will must be biting his nails for your news."

Essex merely flicked his fingers to signal that our strange interview was ended. His eyes had gone suddenly opaque at the old soldier's return. They stared at me emptily, as though I were a stranger, and he made no reply to my murmured farewell.

"I'd hire a linkboy to guide you back," said Sir Roger. "But there are none about."

"The Theatre is barely a quarter mile across the fields," I said. "I can hardly miss it."

Sir Roger walked me to the door. I could have sworn there was a note of distress in his voice when he dismissed me. "Good night, lad," he said. "You'd have made a fine pikeman with those shoulders. Too bad you've set your heart on scribbling—there's little future in the trade."

Only when I stood outside the inn did I recall that I'd been asked there to sup. Instead they had plied me with Spanish wine and served no food at all. For all that, I was treading on air when I took the path to the Theatre. Lights still gleamed in its façade, so I had every hope of finding Master Shakespeare still inside. The news I brought, I dared to hope, would go a long way toward making me a permanent member of the company.

The path across the field was well defined, else I'd have lost my way promptly in the darkness, swigged as I was with drink and the even headier wine of fame. So elevated were my thoughts, in fact, that some time passed before I noticed that the air about me lacked the usual fragrance of the English countryside. In the end I identified the various stenches with a countryman's accuracy—a horsepond on one side of the trail and an open sewer on the other, with a slaughterhouse for hogs just beyond.

Not that I could dwell on such plebeian details tonight. Instead (as is the way with poet and hack alike) I was dreaming busily, forging a play to rival the best that Master Will could pen, with Essex as my backer. Before I had reached the slaughterhouse I had already risen to a high place in court. Why should such a vision prove impossible in this magic age? Was it not true of Essex himself—and of his rival, Sir Walter Raleigh?

I pondered a while on Raleigh, and why his name had come into our conversation at the inn. His rise to fame had been quite as spectacular as that of Robert Devereux—and, if I could believe the records, founded on a far more solid base. An impoverished Dorsetshire gentleman, he had first come to London with little but the shirt on his back and a stout sword arm—enough to earn him a posting to France, to distinguish himself in the wars. A handsome fellow with a devil-may-care approach to life and a stubborn belief in his own destiny, he had come to the Queen's attention upon his return. As I have already noted, he was sent to Ireland to help put down the rebellion. His success in fighting rebels had earned him vast rewards, both there and in England, and he had soon become captain of the Queen's Guard.

From that moment, Raleigh's rise had been phenomenal; almost it had seemed that he could do no wrong. In the end, however, his own headstrong belief in his essential rightness had made him more enemies than one man could dispose of. The ill-starred attempt to plant a colony in that part of the New World he had called Virginia had reduced his prestige. Later, when he had ceased to be the Queen's lover and had dared to marry without her consent, his very neck had been in danger. Though he and his bride had eventually been released from the Tower, Raleigh was said to venture but seldom into the court. (The Virgin Queen, as I have remarked elsewhere, would tolerate no romancing by her former favorites. They must continue to give at least the outward appearance of fidelity, long after they had ceased to fire her blood.)

It was not as a favorite of the Queen that I fancied myself, however, while I strode deeper into the darkness. Unlike Milord Essex, I could hardly picture myself embracing so ancient a bedmate, no matter what the rewards. Rather (if the truth be known), I was reveling in the memory of my romp at the Swan and Dolphin, and scheming ways to arrange a sequel—until I heard a sound on the path ahead that wiped the wine fumes from my brain.

It was only the faintest burr of metal on metal that reached

my ear, but I identified it at once. After all, I'd heard it often
enough that very afternoon on the boards—the sound of a
sword or dagger lifting from its scabbard. And there was just
one reason why cold steel should be drawn on this noisome
pathway tonight. Shawn MacManus (or the purse at his belt)
must be the target.

I stopped dead and asked myself how I could have blundered into such a trap. The purse had hung at my belt when
I'd left the inn—but I'd gone straight down the stairway and
out, so a would-be thief could hardly have outlegged me. Nor
was it logical that a footpad should be lying in wait on this
short cut to the Theatre, now that all traffic from that area
had ceased. The situation was one of complete bafflement—
and it behooved me to think quickly, since I was armed only
with a light dagger.

The news I took to Master Will would keep until morning:
thanks to Essex's purse, I could afford a bed at the inn. So,
with real reluctance (I have never turned my back on a fight
without compelling reasons), I began to retrace my steps. Tomorrow, I promised myself, you'll be properly armed—now
you've had firsthand proof that London is a kennel where dog
eats dog. . . . I could even smile as I blessed my sharp ears and
pictured the cutpurse waiting vainly in the chilly dark.

And then, before I could take a dozen paces, I heard the
same sound. This time, though, the steel had been drawn
somewhere on the pathway that lay between me and the inn.
Not only did an assassin await me near the Theatre; a second
ruffian was dogging my trail, giving me no choice but to stand
and fight two enemies—unless I preferred the sanctuary of
the horsepond or the sewer.

There was gorse beside the path where it sloped to the
pond. I cropped on hands and knees in this convenient ambush until my new enemy could show himself. It was but a
short wait. In another moment I discerned a shadow against
the stars that became chain mail and helmet. It was a man-at-
arms who followed me, with a drawn sword in his fist. Fortunately his eyes were weaker than mine; though he almost
touched me as he passed, I saw that he still imagined me on
the path ahead.

I was upon him in a single pounce, anchoring his sword
arm at wrist and elbow. Smashing a hip against his body to
throw him off balance, I used a lifted knee to snap his

forearm. The bone broke like a dry sapling. The fellow howled with the pain and the weapon slipped from his grasp. With a hand at his scruff, I pivoted and pitched him into the pond.

He was up at once, swimming to the path again, and clutching at his broken arm as he legged it toward the safety of the inn. I let him go with no thought of pursuit. A second enemy waited on the path ahead—and the contest was still far from equal if he, too, was armored. Surprise was the only dodge I could use to advantage. I prepared to employ it before he could interpret the scuffle which I had just won and the howl that ended it.

I moved boldly now, with no effort at concealment, holding the sword before me so the naked blade would catch a glint of starlight. Luck was still with me, for the crunch of my boots on the path and the glimpse of the naked steel lured my second antagonist into speech.

"Is that yer, Matt?"

I grunted an affirmative, careful to keep the sound muted. To my infinite joy, the fellow rose at once from his concealment (less than a dozen yards from the spot where I had taken cover) and I saw that we were of a height. Though he had seen the glint of my sword, he was not quite sure of my location, since I had been careful to drop down the slope to the horsepond, so that I now stood a good three feet below him.

"Stuck 'im proper, eh? I 'eard 'im 'owl."

I was on him before he could draw. Tackling him at the knees in a smashing rush, I threw him backward on the path so violently that I should have stunned him with the first impact. Unfortunately for me, the casque saved his brains from addling; as he crashed to earth, his booted foot caught me squarely on the right wrist, breaking my grip. The pain of the impact lanced through my arm, giving him a chance to wriggle free. Before I could recover my own balance he had drawn his blade and bounced upright.

I saw instantly that he still had to find me in the darkness; and I went under the thrust in a driving lunge before he could brace himself for a second try. The point pinked me just above the knee, but I was past such trifles. This time, when I smashed his skull against the ground, I felt him go limp.

I could have spitted him as he lay there—but I have yet to

kill a man in cold blood and was in no mood for such a re-
venge tonight. Instead, I took him by the heels, braced myself
at the edge of the path, and swung his inert body in an ever-
widening arc, until he was whirling in mid-air at shoulder
level. It is an acrobat's trick I had mastered long ago, permitting me to lift twice my weight. This adversary, a starveling
inside his mail, seemed light as a toy.

Waiting until the rush of air had roused him, I let him
scream twice for mercy before sending him head foremost
into the sewer. Only when he had scrambled to the far bank
and gone howling into the darkness, did I think that I should
have forced out the reason for his attack. Not that I regretted
losing him. For the moment it was enough to pick up both
swords and resume my journey while I reminded myself never
to be so easily cozened again.

At the entrance to the stage alley at the Theatre I felt the
pump of blood at my knee. Even then I did not give myself
time to be afraid. My heady sense of triumph persisted after I
had pushed open the door and reeled onto the empty stage,
faintly lighted by a flambeau in the wings.

"You Irish donkey—who bled you this time?"

The sharp voice seemed to come from nowhere, though I
knew its owner. Holding the two swords in the direction from
which it issued, I struggled for speech—if only to set Master
Will's mind at rest in the matter of Essex's favor. For once,
my tongue refused to function, and the swords clattered to the
stage. I would have fallen with them had not the dramatist
stepped forward to catch me in his arms.

CHAPTER V

Alarums and Excursions

WHEN I opened my eyes it was broad daylight. I
knew that I had not quite fainted after all, despite
my near-collapse.

I lay on a pallet in the sewing room. A low, cheerful hum-
ming nearby told me that Susanna was hard at work. It was
she who had come to help Master Will, when he had shouted

for aid. I recalled how they had placed me here—and how the girl had slit one leg of my trunk hose that she might stitch the wound at my knee and bind it tightly. Afterward she had made me drink a posset of herbs, which had lulled me into a kind of exhausted slumber.

When I lifted my head from the straw ticking that served as a pillow and called to her, Susanna put her task aside and came to stand above me. "If you're still alive, Master MacManus," she said severely, " 'tis only God's mercy. A stuck pig could not have bled more copiously."

"Thank you for saving me, Puss."

"Keep your thanks. You aren't the first brawler whose hide I've repatched." She pushed me back to the pallet as I strove to rise. "Rest a while longer—you're weaker than you know."

"What's the hour?"

"It's past noon. Could you warm your ribs with a bit of broth?"

"I think I could manage," I said. Despite the mockery in her tone, I felt that we were now allies of a sort. "If you'll forgive me for being a nuisance——"

"Who said you were a nuisance? Dick Burbage told you I've a fancy for strays."

After she had gone to fetch the broth I sat up on the pallet to explore the nature of my injury. Thanks to Susanna's stitching, the wound I had suffered seemed only a puckered red welt, though the flesh about it felt tender enough. I had replaced the bandage and resumed my invalid's pose when she returned with a steaming bowl between her hands.

"Aren't you anxious to learn what happened?" I asked, while she spoon-fed me the savory liquid.

"Save your strength, until Master Will arrives," she ordered. "There's no need to waste breath beforehand."

As it happened, we had only a few moments to wait: the playwright's shadow loomed in the doorway before the bowl was quite empty. I had expected him to look down on me with his customary scowl. Instead his voice was gentle as he sat beside the pallet.

"Last night, Master Shawn," he said, "I told Susanna you've a charmed life. Would you agree?"

My hand dropped to the purse at my belt: his eyes followed the gesture even as his shoulders lifted in a shrug.

"What d'you make of it, sir?" I asked.

"It seems Essex was generous."

"He was more than that, Master Will," I said hastily, and described our meeting at the inn, including Milord's promise to recommend yesterday's playbill to the Queen.

The dramatist heard me in silence. "Were you set upon by footpads?"

"So I thought, at first. But both of them were men-at-arms."

"Whose livery did they wear?"

"It was too dark to be sure. But I'll wager they were in the service of Essex."

"Why d'you say that, Irishman?"

"Because I know now that Essex summoned me for a single purpose—to convince himself that I'm the image of someone he knows, and hates."

The dramatist sighed. "In another moment I'll accuse you of stealing my favorite plot."

"It stands to reason, sir," I persisted. "Whoever the person I resemble may be, that resemblance is a threat to Essex. So great a threat that he decided to have me removed before I could endanger him further."

"You're giving yourself delusions, lad. How could you be important to Essex—or to anyone in London?"

"Why else did he invite me to sup—then fuddle me with wine so I'd go maundering into the night? I told you what passed between him and Sir Roger Williams. If what I'm thinking is true, why shouldn't he order my throat cut?"

Master Will took a turn of the sewing room. "Look closely at this yokel, Puss," he ordered. "Does he resemble anyone of importance?"

"God forbid he should have a twin," said Susanna.

"I'm a Stratford man myself," said Shakespeare. "I've only a few London sessions behind me. Dick would be a better judge."

"He's dressing for today's play," said the girl. "I'll summon him."

"Bring your father too. We'll soon find if Master Shawn is raving."

When Burbage appeared he was costumed for the part of Ralph Roister Doister, the braggart soldier of the old comedy of that name. Jaimie Field was close behind him, the prompter's book anchored under one arm, the familiar worry crease between his sandy brows. At sight of me the actor reared back on his heels.

"Who has brought low the captain of the guard?" he asked. " 'Tis a strange end to supper with an earl."

"Tell him, Master Shakespeare," I said, with a glance at Susanna. "My nurse thinks I talk too much."

Both men listened in silence while the playwright repeated my adventure at the inn—and its finale on the path to the Theatre. I will not say that Master Will embroidered my tale, but there was no denying that he told it tautly, with all the flash and thunder of one of his own climaxes. Burbage gave a solemn nod when the story ended, then squatted on his heels beside me and turned my face in profile so the stage keeper could study me.

"Is your guess the same as mine, Jaimie?"

" 'Tis no guess, Master Richard," said Susanna's father. "I should have remarked it yesterday when he wore the uniform —but the play was too much on my mind."

"I'll make the same confession, Will," said Burbage. "They were cast from twin molds."

"By all that's holy—*who?*" asked the playwright.

But the actor would not be cheated. "Twenty years ago," he said, "when he first came to court, Sir Walter Raleigh was this boy's image."

"And a handsome figure young Raleigh cut," added Jaimie Field. "Small wonder the Queen was enamored."

Shakespeare joined the kneeling circle. "You're right, Dick," he said. "What's more, there's still a marked resemblance."

"Come, Puss," said the actor. "You've a sharp pair of eyes. Don't you see it too?"

"I see it, right enough," said Susanna. "But I refuse to bend my knee." And she flounced from the room with her nose held high. I could not help but chuckle at her exit. Accustomed as she was to Burbage's raillery, she could hardly accept the fact that I was now the focus of his attention.

"Tell me, Master Shawn," said the dramatist. "Are you of the same family as Raleigh?"

"Sir Walter's English," I said. "I'm Irish, with a dash of Scotsman."

"That rules out the bloodline. 'Tis a pity: I've used the situation often."

I met his glance squarely. "Give me my part, then," I said. "Else this play must end with but one act. Don't forget the resemblance has already cost me some blood-letting."

Actor and writer exchanged a quick look. "It's unlikely those same two louts will cause you trouble," said Burbage. "Still, it might be wiser to take to earth a while, Master Shawn. You're welcome to hide here, if you like——"

"I didn't cross the Irish Sea to be scared into hiding."

"The boy has spirit," said the actor. "How can we use it, Will?"

"Let's go over what Sir Roger said," the dramatist suggested. "First, he called him the image of Wat—which was Raleigh's nickname, when he first came to court. Sir Roger added, *'He had her in the palm of his hand, then.'* Meaning, of course, that this black stallion might stir up old longings—should the Queen chance to clap eyes on him."

I sat up abruptly, prey to a revulsion I could not name. "If I may speak, gentlemen——"

"They say her passion for Raleigh was like none other," Burbage murmured. "God knows it could revive at the sight of him—"

"Have done!" I shouted. "You've no right to suggest—"

"Take no offense, Shawn MacManus," said Master Will. "Remember, it's a wise father that knows his own child."

"Don't quote your plays to me either," I stormed. "Not if you'd slur my mother's memory." And I glared at him so fiercely he recoiled a bit, with one palm outthrust.

"Let us not argue how the resemblance came about," he told me soothingly. "The important point is that it exists—and may cost you your life. Why not take Dick's advice and return to Cork?"

"Never," I said stoutly.

"Have you a better plan?"

"Not only that: I've the next scene of the play."

The playwright's eyes gleamed. At that moment I saw that I had changed an enemy to a friend. "Let me anticipate it, Shawn," he said. "After all, I'm the scrivener. Since Essex feels you're important enough to kill—you must be still more important to those who oppose him."

"Precisely, sir."

"And you'll hold your ground until you find those allies?"

"With your help," I said, "I'll put myself where they can

see me. On the stage of this theater. Will you risk me in another part?"

Will Shakespeare cast a look at Burbage: I could see that he was more amused than shocked at my effrontery. "What say you, Dick? Shall we see whether this lad is destined for comedy or tragedy?"

"More likely it's the grave," said Burbage. "But there's no denying he'll bring in the crowds, once his story gets around."

"The bargain's made, then," said Master Will. "We'll put you to the fore, Shawn, if I have to write new parts for you."

The day after the brawl I was on my feet again, with only a limp to show for my brush with death, and ready for my coaching. This Susanna gave me, with a grudging competence I resented from the first. Burbage had decided to cast me in small but vivid parts—and it was her task to see that I became letter-perfect in my lines. Since she could parrot the text of almost every play, I hardly blamed her for scolding whenever my woolgathering mind stumbled over a reading. But I could not forgive her antagonism—which seemed to deepen as I grew more proficient.

On the seventh day of my rehearsing, a few hours before I was to go on stage, I finally let my anger explode when she sneered at a rendition for the tenth time. "Hold your tongue, girl," I cried. "You're not training me to succeed Burbage."

"Small chance of that, Master Loudmouth. Take your entrance again—and try not to ogle your audience before you speak."

"I'll take no more entrances. Not until it's time for my performance."

"As you wish," she snapped. "Only pray you'll live that long."

She was standing in the pit with fists clenched and eyes afire. I strode to the edge of the apron and stared down at her in astonishment. For all her raging, her eyes were brimming with tears.

"D'you wish me dead, Puss?" I asked, in a far different tone.

"Of course not. Is it my fault you're too stupid to read the future?"

She tried to escape me after I swung into the pit, dodging

into the first tier of seats, then running like a hare for the stage door. I caught her there and snatched her into my arms.

"Was that stupid too?"

She freed one arm and slapped me with all her strength. This time I pinioned her until she ceased to struggle, lifted her until her brimming eyes were level with mine, and kissed her soundly. I was already a little startled to discover how softly feminine she could be. It was the first time I had thought of her as anything but an impish boy. Now I felt her lips yield under mine, and realized that she was returning my kiss, however briefly—just as a sixth sense informed me, with relentless logic, that she had never been truly kissed before.

"Don't cry, Susanna," I whispered. "Like the cats you've befriended, you'll find I've nine lives."

"Die if you must," she said. "I'll not weep at your funeral." Then she was gone, with her head high and a red flag at each cheek.

I watched her with mixed emotions. My conquest had come about without my knowledge, but the discovery that Susanna Field was enamored of me was no less pleasing for that. In all my twenty years the infinite power of women to surprise me with their ardors had never lost its novelty. There would be time later, I told myself, to complete the seduction. For the present I had weightier matters on my mind.

To my sorrow, I had realized by now that I would never become an outstanding actor—and that my urge to write was but a passing exuberance of youth. The discovery did not sadden me greatly. I still meant to make the theater my life, in the capacity of director or manager, fields which had already come to interest me more. It was enough to feel that I was on terms of real friendship with the company—even with Puss, whose manner toward me underwent a change after our wrestle in the stage door. Home is where the heart is—or so the saying goes. From my first day I had felt I belonged in this raffish milieu, and never once doubted that I would find my niche in time.

Before my reappearance on the boards, Master Will and I had discussed the wisdom of going direct to Raleigh to offer my services—and had decided against it. It was entirely possible that Sir Walter would resent the presence of a double in London: he was still powerful enough to clap me into the Tower if he chose. Besides, we had learned that he was ranging through Dorsetshire at this time, recruiting sailors for the naval patrols that constantly scouted the coasts of Spain.

All in all, I made three appearances at the Theatre without attracting the smallest notice from any quarter, including Milord Essex. I will confess a certain damage to my *amour-propre*—while the days passed in tranquil succession as though I were but one of the dozen starveling mimes who diced and drank in the wings between their scenes. And then, a full fortnight after I received my wound, Jaimie Field approached me after my final exit of the afternoon, and handed me a smudged broadside.

In a way I was prepared for what I read. These sheets (which sold for a penny) were written by anonymous hacks and turned out on presses which were moved the instant their issue was on the streets, the better to escape the wrath of the high-and-mighty folk they libeled so unmercifully.

"Where'd you buy it, Jaimie?"

"From a hawker at Moorgate," said the stage keeper. "They're selling it all over the city."

I could feel my gorge rise as I stared at the heading:

WHAT ABOUT RALEIGH'S BASTARD?

The text was of the same ilk. The broadside spoke of my unmistakable likeness to Sir Walter; the supposition that I must therefore be a natural son of the great man was stated as a fact. Not only did the scurrilous sheet defame my birth (which, as I have stated, was as legitimate as any man's), but it denied me the slightest ability as an actor, referring to me as a stumbling plowboy, a mere mumbler of my lines. Looking back, I will admit this was the unkindest cut in the whole sheet—no doubt, because it was so painfully close to the truth.

I will not deny that the broadside caused an unholy stir. Sir Walter (for all his loss of court favor) was still the symbol of England's greatness, the man who had tweaked King Philip's beard a dozen times, plundered his empire, and intrigued (so far, with no success) to plant Britain's banner on the shores of the New World. Since the captain of the Queen's Guard appeared but seldom in public, that same public now flocked to the Theatre to stare at his facsimile. I cannot deny that I basked in their staring—and waited, with fingers crossed, for the first reaction in high places.

The summons was not long in coming, and I was hardly surprised at its source. Once I held the note in my hand, I wondered why I had not been sent for sooner:

Esteemed Sir:
The writer would be honored if Master Shawn MacManus would accompany the bearer. A matter of importance awaits his attention at the residence of the undersigned.

Pedro de Quesada.

The fact that the note was in Spanish seemed only natural. Like the shadow of Don Pedro's coachman in the stage alley, it belonged to my new-found status. I permitted myself a private chuckle while I stripped off my current costume, donned the best raiment I could filch from our wardrobe press, and stalked out to enter the coach of the envoy from Madrid.

At least I could now translate Quesada's motive in sending for me, as easily as I could understand his pompous prose. By the same token, I could see why he had stared at me on the Oxford road, and his reason for sending Elvira posthaste to my bed at the Swan and Dolphin. . . . If my pulses raced pleasantly as I settled in his splendid equipage and signaled to his coachman to proceed, it was in the hope of a rematch with that knowing siren.

My labors at the Theatre had occupied all my waking moments, so this was my first real view of London—as the coach rumbled through Bishopsgate. I had known, for example, that the ancient, walled-in city described by the poet Chaucer had long since burst its seams at Moorgate and other points, where a dozen sprawling slums were now festering. I had heard of the Royal Exchange (with a hundred shops flourishing under a single roof), of St. Paul's (where the priests dared to conduct their services in English, so long as a Protestant sovereign lived at Whitehall), and of the flood of *émigrés* who had inundated the city with the fall of Antwerp to Philip's armies.

Shawn MacManus, I reflected, was also a foreigner of sorts. As an Irishman, I was immediately suspected of all manner of traitorous feelings, whether or not I indulged in open acts of treason. The Theatre (where I had been received with such easy camaraderie) was a world apart. My real testing would come today, when I set foot in the metropolis of the English universe. Yet I assured myself that I would be given a fair trial here, until I had proved my worth. Elizabeth's England was a forward-looking land, a country in yeasty ferment, where new ideas bubbled in every brain, and each man, regardless of race or creed, might scrawl his name large on the next page of history.

I studied the crowded streets eagerly, half hoping for a glimpse of one of those red aborigines Raleigh had caused to be brought from his ill-fated colony in the New World— though reason told me these copper-hued savages had long since vanished from London. At least my ears were able to verify a story I had only half believed, namely that one could hear a half dozen tongues spoken in the course of a few blocks' journey in the commercial center of the town. It was even said that a man could learn any known language from a tutor born in that very land (whether it be Arabic, Dutch, Polish, Turkish, Russian, or French), for the sum of a shilling a week—but this was a tale I was not, as yet, prepared to credit.

All in all, it was a lusty, growing city that Quesada's coach traversed en route to his residence at Thames-side. I have already remarked that the homes of the wealthy were situated on the bank of that noble river, each in its green setting of garden. Quesada's manse stood above a short flight of steps that dropped to the water, within a stone's toss of Whitehall itself—near enough, I told myself, for the ready transmission of palace secrets, for it was common knowledge that the dons had informers everywhere.

When the coach deposited me before the brass-studded door (with the Spanish coat of arms on the keystone above it) I stood for an instant before lifting the knocker, like a fox flairing a trap. Nor did I neglect to cross myself when a butler in yellow-and-gold livery bowed me across a great tiled courtyard to a *sala* hideous with looped velvet, full suits of armor, and hidalgos in a dozen gilded frames. King Philip's chief agent lived well indeed, it seemed, but the total effect of this splendor was somehow funereal. I was considerably relieved when the hangings parted and Elvira herself came into my waiting arms.

The kiss she gave me had all its remembered quality; the hands that caressed me briefly—before the girl could free herself from my ardors—brought back flaming memories of that night in Oxford, along with a host of brand-new hungers.

"There is no time for more, *querido*——" I had already followed her into the embrasure of a window to exact a second kiss. "My uncle is expected at any moment."

"Must we speak of *him?*"

"No more—please. It is enough to know you have not forgotten me."

"Muy encantadora—I love you more than life itself." I have stated elsewhere that such a speech takes on added fire in Castilian—but even Dick Burbage, I am sure, would have applauded my delivery. "When do I see you again, *Elvira mía?*"

"That's hardly for me to say."

"I can't call here without Don Pedro's permission."

"You'll be invited often enough," she said. "Surely you already know he means to use you."

Shocked though I was by her unexpected avowal, I kept my poise. "Frankly, my dearest," I said, "I hoped *you'd* be using me."

"So I will, Señor Shawn."

"As you used me in Oxford?"

"I might arrange it," she said calmly. "If you'll swear to be careful."

"Try me."

Again she avoided my embrace. "Our coachman is called Enrique," she said. "Give him a shilling now and again: you'll find him useful."

"How so?"

"I'll send him to the Theatre to fetch you—the moment it's safe for you to spend the night." She lowered her eyes modestly—as though to atone, in some measure, for her brazen words—then lifted a key on its chain from her bodice and tossed it to me. "This will open the door to the water gate. No one need see you come or go——"

"The water gate will be my portal to Paradise," I said, in that same useful Spanish. "Let us hope I'm worthy to unlock it."

"You proved your worth—at the Swan and Dolphin." She moved toward the door on that, with the chuckle that had already raised such havoc in my blood. "If our luck holds, Enrique will be calling before the week is out." I rushed to claim her lips for a farewell kiss, but she was gone, with a prodigious rustle of petticoats.

Alone in the *sala* once more, I composed myself with an effort. Her performance, I reflected, had been perfect—so perfect, in fact, it was a wrench to remind myself that she was but a pawn in King Philip's service. Until my heart could steady, I moved again to the window, to stare down at a wide vista of the river, and a barge that was warping into the royal landing stage. . . . I was still there, fighting hard to compose my breathing, when Don Pedro de Quesada bustled in at the door.

"Welcome to our house, Señor MacManus," said the rogue, in his lisping Spanish. "I regret that affairs of office have postponed this meeting."

"I also, señor."

"Last Friday I attended the play with Milord Cecil. May I compliment your performance?"

"You are too kind, Don Pedro. I've much to learn as an actor."

"At least you've achieved your wish." He led me to a couch. At a single imperious handclap, his major-domo entered with a wine service. "I take it you enjoy the confidence of Master Burbage?"

"And Will Shakespeare," I said. " 'Tis a real privilege to study with the greatest poet of our time."

"Do you still hope to surpass him one day?"

"Not since I've heard his lines spoken on the boards."

"Yet you mean to be a poet in your own right?"

I spoke carefully; after all, I had reasons for keeping my mooncalf role. "Yes, señor—if I can find subjects to my liking."

"Poets are admired in Madrid; in fact, most of them are under the King's protection."

"Which means they must write to please His Majesty?"

"What else?"

"I'd not endure that, señor. I came to London to do as I please."

The Spaniard shrugged. "The English make a cult of their independence. In Spain we pride ourselves on loyalty to the throne."

"An Irishman prides himself on loyalty to his own fortunes," I said. It was my new attack in the scene—one of the first dramatic tricks that Master Will had taught me. "That's why we'll never knuckle under to England."

"Haven't you done just that—by coming to London?"

"After all, señor, I'm not the first rebel to regroup his forces."

So far we had only been feeling each other out. When Quesada put down his wineglass I sensed that I had passed my first test. "I'll be frank, Señor MacManus," he said. "During the past fortnight my agents in Ireland have checked the story you told at the Swan and Dolphin. They speak well of your veracity."

"Why should you have cause to doubt me?"

"*Amigo mío*, I am about to make you an unusual offer. I cannot risk a misunderstanding." With the words, he opened a desk drawer and extracted the broadside that celebrated my resemblance to Raleigh.

"How much of this is true?"

I kept my dignity. "That's not for me to say, Don Pedro. If your Irish agents earned their keep, they've informed you that my birth is as legal as your own."

"Sir Walter served in that part of Ireland as the Queen's officer. He *could* be your natural father."

"So he could," I said. "Just as the Emperor Charles might have fathered *you* before he sired your present King. Have done, sir—and remember, I'll call out any man who dubs me bastard to my face."

I had expected him to bridle over this sneer. Instead he only grinned. "You speak as a gentleman and a loyal son," he murmured. "I commend your spirit. The fact remains that your resemblance to Raleigh is astonishing. I noticed it at once, when we met on the highroad——"

"Is that why you persuaded me to dine at the inn?"

"Did you think I asked you because your back was strong enough to lift my coach?"

I poured myself a fresh bumper of wine without waiting for him to offer it. "Tell me more, Don Pedro," I said.

"What d'you know of the New World? Or should I say, New Spain?"

The question confused me. The dons are famous for their serpentine approach, and this one seemed typical of his race. "Little enough," I said truthfully.

"Spain's whole future depends on the New World. It's ours, by right of discovery and conquest. We'll never share it with England."

"You claim it all?"

"From the equator to the pole."

"What of the voyages of the Cabots? I've heard that they explored the coast of Florida—as far as Cuba."

I saw the furnace door open in his busy brain. "Who told you of the Cabots?"

"I read of their explorations years ago."

"If the Cabots claim the Floridas for England, they lie. Florida extends from the Cuban strait to the limits of the northern seaboard. It includes the lands called Virginia— where Raleigh once tried to found a colony."

"It's a point I'm not prepared to argue."

"Master Shawn, the English are a restless race—and they have found their sea legs. Spain must defend its domain against them."

"Are Englishmen planning settlements on your borders?"

"Spain has no borders in the New World. We're prepared to repel all strangers, including Raleigh."

I pricked up my ears at this. Sir Walter had irons in many fires. Only two years ago he had helped capture the *Madre de Dios*, a Spanish galleon groaning with plunder. I had heard he was using this sum to finance a new expedition to America (the same area that Quesada had described, no less vaguely, as Florida). I had paid little heed to those rumors. To my mind, the whole New World was Outer Barbaria.

"Raleigh has failed once," I told Quesada. "Why should he try again?"

"Who can say what Raleigh will do next? This much is certain: one of his lieutenants has recently scouted the Caribbean. We know that he explored the shores of Trinidad, and the Guiana coast. Now we're told that Raleigh is outfitting a fleet at Plymouth and recruiting settlers among the poor in London. It is also said that he plans to take Trinidad as his preserve—that he'll use it as a base while he searches for a route to El Dorado."

"Did you say *El Dorado?*" My spirits had leaped as I uttered the words. The myth of Manoa—and the "Golden Ones" who ruled there as princes—was familiar to every schoolboy. Who could believe a tale of red-skinned potentates who dusted their bodies with powdered gold? Yet El Dorado, whether man or region, must exist somewhere, judging by the tons of precious metal Spain had brought from the New World.

Quesada spoke in an English devoid of accent. "I see you know the legend."

"Isn't it more than that? I've even heard that El Dorado lies somewhere on the headwaters of the Orenoque—the river which empties into the sea near Trinidad."

The Spaniard frowned. "You are as well informed as most, Master Shawn. It hardly matters if the story is true or false. The Orenoque is part of New Spain. Or will be when we've promoted treaties with the caciques, who are overlords of that region."

"What if Raleigh makes treaties first?"

I had baited him deliberately, if only to lure him into a little plain speaking—and was rewarded when a flush mounted to his cheeks. "That is what we must prevent. If you'll help, I'll make it worth your while."

I breathed deep before I spoke; this was my first real hurdle. "What service did you have in mind?"

"Have you seen Raleigh—or had orders from him?"

"No, señor."

"Or sent him word, on your own part?"

"Hardly, when I'm still unsure of my welcome."

Quesada nodded. "That was wise of you. Let him make the first move, Señor Shawn: he's bound to, once he's read this broadside. Knowing the man, I'm positive he'll offer you a place in his entourage——"

"Why, Don Pedro?" I asked, making my face bland as a two-year-old's.

"To have you on his side, of course."

"Meaning that I might embarrass him if I joined another faction?"

"*Precisamente.* If Raleigh offers such a post, will you take it?"

I kept my boyish grin. "I'd be a fool to refuse it."

"You could go far with such a man—perhaps even to the New World."

"You just said you'd deny us entrance there."

"His Catholic Majesty realizes we cannot patrol our whole

shore line. It's possible that Raleigh intends only to plant a second colony in Virginia. We'd let such a venture go unmolested—at least for the present. The Caribbean and the Main are a different story. So are the approaches to Manoa, the country of the Golden Ones——"

"But you feel the Golden Ones are myths, Don Pedro."

"There are two schools of thought in Madrid. One of them, and it's close to the King, believes there *are* cities of gold in the Orenoque basin. In any event, we'll soon be exploring the whole region and annexing it to our present domains."

"And if the English have the same plan——?"

"Then we will summon all our resources and destroy them. Do I make myself clear?"

"Clear enough, for now." I got to my feet, anxious to terminate this visit while the initiative was still mine. "First, I'm to gain Raleigh's confidence. *Then* I'm to act as informant."

"Would you find the task distasteful?"

"When I'm in London to make my fortune?"

"You'll be well paid, señor."

"Such work would deserve high pay."

"Naturally we'll wait until Raleigh takes notice of you."

I kept my face straight, while my fingers caressed Elvira's key, which I had prudently concealed in my doublet. "When do we meet again?"

"After you've joined forces with Sir Walter. There's no reason for an earlier conference."

So the old goat had no intention of mentioning his niece at this time. Elvira's task, it appeared, was even simpler than mine—to keep my interest pinned where it belonged.

"What if Raleigh never summons me?" I asked.

"Then we've wasted an hour to no purpose," said Quesada tartly. "Surely a man of your age can squander that much time."

He dismissed me then, with a certain coldness—as though, belatedly, he had decided not to seem eager. His butler was given the privilege of showing me to the door. On the stoop, I waved the coachman aside and half circled the house until I had marked the location of the water gate, and the half-hidden portal just above the river steps. Perhaps it was only my fancy, but I felt sure that Elvira's eyes were upon me as I set my cap at a raffish angle and strolled down the Strand.

A hundred yards beyond Quesada's door I realized I was being followed. This time my pursuers were four in number. Night had begun to fall, but there was enough afterglow from the river to warn me that these were members of the Queen's Guard. It was equally obvious that they had posted themselves near the Spaniard's manse and had only awaited my departure to arrest me.

I set my back to the nearest wall and drew my dagger—but the leader of the group, an ox in chain mail, only laughed as his companions closed in.

"Put back your weapon, lad," he said. "Are you Master Shawn MacManus?"

"That I am," I growled. "What's your business with me?"

"You'll see presently. Just march along—and look lively."

I marched, having no choice. Since these were Queen's men, I could think only of Essex: it seemed he had experienced a change of heart and meant to jail me for the beating I had given his lackeys. At least I could take pride in my captors: only prisoners of note were taken by Elizabeth's own guard.

My fears deepened as we followed the river for a while, took a few cobbled turnings, then entered the portals of a noble dwelling whose chimney pots seemed to blot out the stars.

"What place is this?" I demanded.

"Durham House," said my chief warden. "You *are* a country lad."

The name meant nothing, but I was careful to hide my ignorance as they marched me up a stairway to a turreted study, book-lined from floor to ceiling and warm with the light of a brisk fire.

"Wait here," said my jailer. "The captain will see you in a moment."

They left me, without a word of explanation—a quartet that knew its business and would brook no complaints from strangers. I made a quick survey of the room, if only to assure myself that the windows were unbarred: Durham House was no part of that dread prison-fortress called the Tower. My heart had quieted somewhat, though my gorge was still high, when the door opened behind me. I turned to face a tall, black-bearded man in dusty traveling clothes, who had paused on the threshold and was studying me thoughtfully.

It was Sir Walter Raleigh. I had never encountered him before, but the recognition was mutual.

CHAPTER VI

Sir Walter Raleigh

I KNEW him instantly, as I have said—and for the most cogent of reasons. No act of recognition could have gone deeper. Looking into those brown eyes (even when they were snapping with anger) was like finding myself in a conjurer's mirror. It was an older face but it was still mine— and the world had carved its own heavy pattern there.

For the first time I could really understand why Quesada had stared—and why Essex had turned pale when I made my entrance at the playhouse.

Raleigh walked to a writing table that stood on the far side of the tower room. He seated himself behind it, still without speaking; the silence between us had begun to grow intolerable before the bearded lips parted.

"Well, young man? What can you say for yourself?"

I had committed no crime, so far as he was concerned, and I felt my backbone stiffen. "I've nothing to say," I replied just as harshly. "Not until I know of what I'm accused."

"Accused?" The word choked in his throat and he seemed too enraged to continue. "Is it not enough that I return from the Queen's business to find you posing as my bastard?"

The charge was false, of course, and I gave him the lie direct. "I made no such claim! Don't say things you can't prove, sir."

"Who are you, then?"

"I'm called Shawn MacManus—and I was born in wedlock. I'll match my bloodline with yours."

The counterattack, it seemed, had rocked him on his heels, though his voice was still as bitter as the laughter. "I should have known that only an Irishman would carry off this hoax."

"I came to London to earn my bread," I told him, "which I'm doing at Master Burbage's theater. Is it any fault of mine that I resemble you?"

Raleigh leaned forward and selected a clay pipe from the table. Silence built between us while he tamped the bowl with a shaggy brown herb and lighted it from the grate. This, I gathered, was tobacco; the smoking of it had been taught him by the aborigines from Virginia.

"So you resemble me," he said. "D'you hope to profit from the fact?"

"Nothing was further from my thoughts until Essex sent for me."

"Then it was Essex who ordered the broadside written."

"I consider it most unlikely that Essex ordered it. Not when his lackeys had already made an attempt on my life."

"What nonsense are you telling me now?"

"It's no nonsense, sir. If you'll compose yourself, I'll try to explain."

Sir Walter blew smoke through both nostrils and sank back in his chair, puffing mightily on his pipe until the vapors he exhaled all but obscured him from my view. I remembered hearing that his servant—coming upon him for the first time while he was smoking tobacco—had doused him with water, thinking him on fire. At this moment I could understand the fellow's action.

"You have your audience, lad," he said. "Give your performance and, for your own sake, make it convincing."

I told the story from the beginning, from my first view of the Theatre to the encounter on Finsbury Fields. I will not deny that I made my own case as heroic as I could, but I did not embroider the tale with supposition. When I finished I saw at once that he believed me.

"Be sure of one thing, Master Shawn MacManus." His tone had softened from its former brusqueness. "This resemblance will probably cost you your life if you remain in London."

"I'm here to make my fortune, sir. No man can drive me out—not if you'll support me."

"You're asking my help, then?"

"If you're free to give it."

"Why should I lift a finger?"

"No reason at all, beyond common humanity—and the fact that nature has minted us from the same die."

"What part of Ireland d'you hail from?"

"I was born near Cork, sir."

"Is your mother Irish?"

"She was called Jane Barry."

The pipestem snapped in his hand. This time, when he raised his head, he looked at me directly. I could not tell if he liked what he saw.

"And your father?"

"He was named Alfred MacManus—a squire of our district."

"Are your parents living?"

"I'm an orphan, sir—an older half brother has inherited the estate. That's why I'm searching for a career."

"You've asked my help," he said. "Suppose I offered it?"

"I'd try to deserve your patronage."

"What of this game with Quesada?" he asked. "Will you play it my way?"

"So far," I said, "it's the Spaniard who has played games, not I."

"We're aware of Quesada's motives at Whitehall," he said. "So far, we've countered them. Will you explain how he means to use you—or shall I?"

"Perhaps it's my turn to listen, sir."

"He has informers at Plymouth. Everyone in England knows I plan another voyage to the New World the moment the Queen gives me leave to go. All that's in doubt is my destination. *That's* the best-kept secret in the realm, for the best of reasons. In the end it will be Elizabeth Tudor who decides."

He puffed for a moment, while his eyes turned to a far horizon he would never share. When he spoke again he seemed half forgetful of my presence. "So far, the New World is too big for men's minds to grasp. The dons have done no more than scratch its surface."

"Surely the gold of the Incas can't be dismissed so lightly."

"The real wealth of America lies elsewhere," he said. "It won't be discovered in my day, or yours. But it's time we staked out our claim if we're to exploit it later. At least that's the argument I'd offer the Queen if I could gain an audience——"

"Would you plant another colony in Virginia?" I asked.

"Virginia or the Guiana coast—how can I know until I've seen both? Meanwhile, the real question remains unanswered —do we go for gold or settlement? No man can read the Queen's mind: it's changeable as quicksilver, and as elusive.

It's my guess she'll vote for gold: she's a lifetime worshiper of El Dorado."

"Quesada thinks you'll sail for Guiana."

"And he expects you to confirm his judgment? Have I guessed his game rightly?"

"To the life."

There was no feeling of strain between us now; this time, the bearded lips above the pipestem just missed smiling. "As an Irishman," he said, "you've the right to choose. I could hardly fault you if you cast your lot with Spain. There's a Bible on that shelf. Will you swear you're the Queen's man—now and forever?"

I took up the Book, and stood eye to eye with him before his hearth fire. "Now and forever, Sir Walter," I said. "So help me God."

"Let's hope you never regret those words."

"I've stood up to Essex," I reminded him. "What's one risk more?"

"Naturally I'll protect you. But you must use your own wits where Don Pedro—and that doxy he calls his niece—are concerned."

"I think I can manage, sir."

"With your Irish heritage, I suspect you're right. The Spaniards and I are old antagonists; we can even read each other's minds. I knew Quesada would use you the moment I read that broadside. If he hasn't already employed the lovely Elvira to keep you docile, he's sure to do so. Play your cards well. You may find the bondage pleasant."

"I've no cause to complain," I said.

"See that there's no change. And if you spend a full night between Doña Elvira's sheets, try not to talk in your sleep."

"So far she's given me little chance for slumber."

"We need slander Señorita Quesada no further then," he said. "Actually she isn't the baggage she seems: I'm told she has antecedents in Madrid—and that she's the ward of the present governor of Trinidad. So her interest in my future is no less ardent than her uncle's."

"I'll bear that in mind, sir."

Raleigh rose from his chair and knocked the ashes from his pipe. "I've no more to tell you now, Shawn," he said, and the use of my Christian name seemed quite natural. "I'll consult soon with my advisers and decide on our next move. In the meantime it's essential that you remain alive. As a proof of my good intentions I am going to assign you a bodyguard."

"I'd be honored, sir," I murmured. Events had moved at a headlong pace today, and I was still a trifle breathless—but that flourish was part of Raleigh, part of the incisive brain that swept all before it to attain its chosen end. Had he rubbed the lamp on his writing table and produced a djin from the empty air to do his bidding, I would not have been too startled. As it was, he merely touched a bellpull and gave an order to a servant. In another moment I stood face to face with a square-shouldered, copper-dark man of my own age and brawn, who embarrassed me instantly by dropping to one knee and kissing my hand.

"This is Pablo," my host explained. "He's an Indian from the Orenoque valley; Captain Whiddon brought him back when I sent him exploring. In the interval, I've taught him English. You'll find him prepared to defend you with his life."

"As the señor wishes," said Pablo. It was a statement of intention, made without heroics. In the same spirit I bade him rise to his feet again and grasped his hand firmly in my own. He was the first red man I had seen in the flesh (though his accent told me that he was partly of Spanish blood). What surprised me most of all was the fact that I knew him instantly for a friend.

"I'm afraid I've no place for you at the Theatre," I said, remembering my cramped quarters in the sewing room.

"He needn't attend you there," said Raleigh. "I doubt if Essex would try to murder you in the preserves of the Lord Chamberlain's own company. I'll arrange to quarter Pablo at an ordinary; he'll be a pace behind you whenever you venture outside. Believe me, it's a wise precaution."

I stood a little aside while he gave the Indian his instructions. The fact that Pablo wore the garb of an Englishman seemed no less bizarre than the *pistolas* in his belt. I had thought all aborigines went mother-naked, armed only with spears and arrows.

"If it's New World lore you're after," said Raleigh, "Pablo knows more of Guiana than any man in London." He drew a sailing chart from the drawer. "We'll meet here tomorrow, Shawn. What's the bill at the Theatre?"

"They're giving *Henry VI* again, sir."

"I've heard of that play," said Raleigh. "Will's a good man and I'd like to see him in it. What part d'you take?"

"The captain of the guard."

"I don't doubt you'll cut a fine figure. If I can't attend in person, my coach will call for you: I'll want you to dine here with me and meet a personage you'll be none the worse for knowing."

"Thank you again, sir—for everything."

"Perhaps it's you who should be thanked, when this business is behind us." His sign of dismissal was almost brusque. That, too, was Raleigh's way. He was never a man to waste time, once a course was charted.

CHAPTER VII

A Challenge to a Duel

NEXT MORNING, wolfing a late breakfast of ale and sausage before rehearsal, I was hard put to believe that yesterday's events were real. It was still harder to curb my eager tongue when Susanna chided me on my absence. I could hardly explain my *entretien* with Quesada. Certainly I could not yet boast of an alliance which Raleigh himself had not made public.

A glance into the stage alley—where Pablo stood with folded arms and a wary eye for all comers—convinced me that I had not been dreaming. Later, watching the Theatre fill, my heart almost burst with pride when Raleigh appeared in the lower balcony, just before the heralds' trumpets sounded.

His entrance brought a thundering cheer from the groundlings. It was the final proof (though I needed none) that he remained the people's favorite. It was a stirring thing to watch how graciously he accepted the applause, bowing to right and left as the storm spread to the last seat. Dick Burbage, about to make his entrance, waited for the din to subside, lest his lines be drowned out—and even Puss, standing beside me with the prompt board, watched with admiring eyes.

Susanna was not portraying Joan this afternoon, but the slender boy who took the role was more than adequate. In fact, the whole performance went admirably, as though each actor, basking in the sunshine of Raleigh's interest, could not fail to give his best. In the intervals, there was a constant procession of noble folk to the area where he sat, for all the world like a prince of the blood at his levee. Watching them come and go, I wondered which among them was the personage with whom I had been bidden to dine at Durham House.

The moment my brief scene was over, I hastened to the sewing room to don the best costume I could find for our meeting. Pablo was waiting in the alley and dropped a dutiful step behind as I hastened into the crowd to find Sir Walter's carriage. The press was thick at the lane where the coaches waited; I'll confess that I was not too careful in my hurry. When an elbow caught my midriff, so sharply that I was almost bowled over, I needed the Indian's hand at my elbow to save me from falling. At the same instant I found myself facing a dandy in blue velvet, whose hand was already on his sword.

"Watch where you're going, ruffian!" he snarled.

I knew he had struck me deliberately, but I kept my temper. Eager as I was to find Sir Walter, I had no desire for a brawl. "I'm sorry if I disturbed you, sir," I said courteously —and made to move on toward the carriages.

"You pushed me," he said. "I have witnesses."

Pablo came forward as the fellow continued to finger his sword, but I signaled to him to keep back. "Truly you're mistaken, sir," I said. "No doubt the press of the crowd threw us together."

"Are you giving me the lie? I say you jostled me."

"And I still say you're mistaken." Without taking my eyes from that dead-white face, I knew that a hundred expectant playgoers had clustered around us—eager, as always, to encourage a fight in the making.

"No man can call me a liar twice," the popinjay screamed in a voice that was oddly womanish, now that his temper had burst all bounds. Then he slapped me with a ringed hand, opening a cut under my right eye. Too late, I realized that he had stalked me to force a challenge, and that the stalking had been on order. Certainly this was no ordinary, catch-as-catch-can quarrel: from his wire-muscled frame to the length of his sword, the man had the look of a dueling master.

Again I restrained Pablo. Bracing my feet, I swung a fist from my knees and connected solidly with the fellow's chin. I saw his eyes go glassy as he went sprawling. In other circumstances the look on his face would have been ludicrous. In fact, there was a concerted guffaw from the onlookers when he tottered to his feet at last and tested the hinges of his jawbone.

"You'll die for this, MacManus," he said, as he spat out a tooth. "My seconds will call on you tonight."

I could hardly decline the challenge with the eyes of the crowd upon me. Obviously this was a hired bravo who had done his crude best to make me call him out. His only mistake had been his failure to reckon with the temper of a countryman accustomed to using his fists. Thus, despite himself, he had been provoked into issuing the challenge.

My assailant was still breathing fire—and brushing the mud from his doublet—when the crowd parted and a familiar voice broke in on our mutual defiance.

"What's your game this time, Fitzraugh?"

It was Raleigh—and the question, barked into the dandy's face, explained everything. This was Sir Harlan Fitzraugh, an aide to Milord Essex and one of the best swordsmen in England. Even in Cork his name was well known: it was said that he had fought over a score of duels, most of which had ended fatally for his opponents.

"You're a little late, Sir Walter," said Fitzraugh. "I've already marked your bastard for extinction."

Raleigh, I saw, was putting a checkrein on his own temper as well as mine. Just in time he seized my wrist, stopping a blow that would have finished my enemy for the day. "I've no quarrel with you, Fitzraugh," he said. "And I'll have the guard on you if you pick another. What was his excuse, Shawn?"

No one stirred as I told my side of the story—rejoicing, the while, at the way the dandy's jaw was puffing.

"Who gave the challenge?" asked Raleigh.

"He did, sir."

"Then you've no choice but to accept," said Sir Walter. His shoulders sagged as he uttered the pronouncement: despite my own despair, I was pleased that he had taken my courage for granted.

"Will you be my second, sir?"

"Of course—if you wish it. You're the challenger, Fitzraugh. Master MacManus will name the weapons."

The fencing master shrugged. "I'll fight with any choice of blades."

"We'll settle details when your seconds call at Durham House," said Raleigh. "Come, Shawn, we've a dinner engagement." He turned on his heel and strode through the crowd. I put down the urge to smash a second blow into the sneering face of my challenger and followed, with Pablo dogging our footsteps.

Raleigh said but little on the drive into London, giving me ample time to digest the fruits of my folly. Had I waited in the Theatre, the trap could not have been sprung. Now, with all except the details of my legal murder completed, it seemed I had little more future than a criminal condemned to the block.

"Don't blame me too much, sir," I said finally. "I hardly thought they'd strike so soon."

"Essex must have learned of our meeting and felt time was pressing," said Raleigh. "This won't be the first occasion Fitzraugh has served as his executioner."

"Does he fear you so much, then?"

"Of course. What's more, he knows just how I mean to use you. Providing—as I said yesterday—I can find some means of keeping you alive." With that cryptic pronouncement Raleigh settled in his corner of the coach and said no more until we had rumbled into the courtyard of Durham House.

"Can you handle a rapier, Shawn?" he asked as the equipage came to a stop.

"I'm no fencing master," I admitted. "The French dueling sword is too light for my hands."

"Don't be too gloomy, lad," he told me. "There must be a solution to this dilemma—we've only to find it." His butler was already bowing at the carriage door. With an abrupt gesture, Raleigh pushed tomorrow aside and focused his mind on the present.

"Sir Robert Cecil is here, sir."

"Good—we'll wait on him directly."

Despite the dominance of Milord Essex in certain quarters, there was no man the Queen trusted more than Cecil. At this moment his power was almost as great as his father's, when the elder Cecil had been King of England in all save name. I was glad to note that Raleigh entered the house with the air of a man who refused to spell out the bitter letters of failure. I understood why, when I caught sight of the slender, slightly bowed figure in the hall.

Sir Robert Cecil, I observed instantly, had an air of authority that matched Raleigh's—a quiet determination that could not be gainsaid. It was a quality hard to put into words. Looking back on that meeting now, I realize it was only the intangible stuff of which every true leader is made. In Cecil's case the leadership was, of necessity, veiled. Yet he was a man who, without bombast or vainglory, usually got precisely what he wanted.

When Sir Walter introduced me, I had no way of knowing whether he would endorse my meeting with Fitzraugh. If he did, I told myself (with a sudden, unreasonable rise of spirits), my chance of survival would be considerably increased. Raleigh was the urbane host from our first words, calling for wine and leading us to the dining salon with a flourish. During the first courses of the elaborate meal, he gave Sir Robert a running account of my adventures, including my meetings with Quesada. Cecil's eyes sparkled as Sir Walter outlined his plan of action in that quarter—and clouded, just as decisively, when he heard of the challenge.

"It's a personal affair, Wat," he said. "I can't intervene."

"Fitzraugh was given his orders by Essex or Williams—it makes no difference which."

"He knew my name," I volunteered. "Though I'd never seen him before."

Cecil studied me under knitted brows. "You can still go back to Ireland with a whole skin," he said. "No one who knows Essex will blame you."

"I'm not afraid to fight him, sir. Not if we can meet on equal terms."

"You've the choice of weapons?"

"Fortunately."

At the table's head, Raleigh was lost in thought. "You can hardly name a weapon with which Fitzraugh is not adept," he said. "It's no secret that he once conducted a fencing school."

Sir Robert nodded. "I'm a fair swordsman myself, but I'd as soon face one of your Scottish knights, armed with that barbarous broadsword they call a claymore."

The word exploded in my brain. I got to my feet so violently that I overturned my wineglass. "You've saved my life, Sir

Robert," I shouted—knowing he was certain I'd gone daft. Raleigh, however, caught my meaning at once.

"You'll never find claymores in London, Shawn," he said.

"We've several at the Theatre," I told him, my voice still trembling from the joy of this reprieve. "Only yesterday I was showing Dick Burbage their use—for a play he's planning about King Macbeth of Scotland."

Raleigh clapped his hands for more wine. "Then we've a real surprise for Sir Harlan tomorrow. No one deserves it better." He put the matter aside with one of his imperious gestures and began to discuss his forthcoming voyage with Sir Robert. But I could see that his confidence in my survival had been restored, as it were, in a single bound.

As I expected, Cecil agreed readily to our plan for hoodwinking Quesada. It was decided that I should visit the Spaniard freely while preparations for the voyage to the New World developed—and insist that Raleigh was proceeding with his original plan to take settlers to the Virginia country. What with the wine (which continued to flow freely until midnight) and the glittering plans of these two fine gentlemen, my head was whirling when Sir Cecil took his leave at last. Fitzraugh's seconds had long since been received and sent about their business, which was to set the place of tomorrow's meeting and inform my adversary that I would bring the weapons for our encounter. On the stroke of twelve I was bundled off to bed in a chamber adjoining the tower study, where I fell, at long last, into an uneasy slumber.

It seemed no more than the closing of an eyelid before Pablo was tugging at my counterpane. A special, dead-black costume was waiting at the bedside, the duelist's garb that punctilio demanded. Sir Walter was similarly attired when we met in the hall. Dawn was just breaking outside, but we would have a long ride to pick up the weapons at the Theatre and must traverse London a second time to reach the place of combat.

Despite the early hour, Susanna was busy in the sewing room when I entered. "This morning, it seems that our tomcat returns with the sunrise," she said tartly—but I caught a gleam of concern in her eye that belied her airy insult.

"I told you I'd be dining with Sir Walter," I said. "He kept me afterward."

She lifted the folds of my doublet, testing its texture with her seamstress's fingers. "Is it true you're fighting a duel today?"

"In Southwark—within the hour."

"See that you come back whole, in time for the performance," she ordered. "I'll not patch another wound."

"What if I don't return at all?"

"Then we'll make do with another apprentice. One thing is certain at the Theatre, Master Blarney, there's never a shortage of actors."

I did not press the point but went instead to open one of the chests where the armor was kept. "Stand by to cue my first entrance, Puss," I said. "We've a surprise in store for Fitzraugh." As I spoke I lifted one of the claymores from its bed of oiled rags and swung it about my head in a dazzling arc. "I'll wager he never fought with one of these."

"Have you?"

"Often. It's by way of being a national weapon."

Susanna had backed away while I hefted the huge blade. She approached me again after I had encased both weapons in their wrappings. "They seem as clumsy as you," she said. "And just as formidable."

"Let us hope Sir Harlan finds them so." This time she did not withdraw when I put an arm about her. "I must fight the only way I can, Puss—God knows I'm no knight. I'd still like a favor from my lady to wear into this joust."

"Your lady?"

"I won't call you my guardian angel. But you've been a bit of both. Your hair ribbon, perhaps?"

"My hair's too short for ribbons."

"Your garter then?"

I'd expected her to bridle at the impertinence. Instead she withdrew from my embrace and lifted her skirt. I had a glimpse of milk-white flesh before she straightened with a fancy garter in her hand. It was something I would never have suspected her of wearing, a thing of lace as dainty as a mountain flower.

"See you bring it back," she said.

"If I do—may I put it on?"

There was mischief in her eyes this time, as well as a hint of tears. When she came forward to kiss me I had to lift her by both elbows, so great was the difference in our height. "You'll find *that* out when the time comes, Master Knight," she said, and slapped me, not too hard, when I tried to capitalize on the fleeting caress. "Now off you go to battle. Sir Walter isn't used to waiting."

She ran out on that, and I watched her go, with an odd stirring of the pulses, something infinitely different from the usual tingle after such sport. It was not my first tussle with Puss; each time, I remembered, I had felt the same afterglow. But there was no time to ponder such matters as I hurried out to rejoin Raleigh.

In the coach he insisted on unwrapping both claymores and examining them thoroughly.

"They bring back the charges of your Irish knights during the rebellion," he said, running his finger along the edge of the blade. "If you're to kill Fitzraugh with this, you must beat him to death—or split his skull."

"I don't plan to kill him, sir. Not if I can avoid it."

"He'll kill you if he gets the chance. Those are his orders."

"I'm not forgetting that either."

The area on the south bank of the Thames was known as the Liberty of the Clink, since it was outside the jurisdiction of the London council and controlled by the Queen herself. Not that Elizabeth favored dueling within the court. It was a solemn fact that more than one swashbuckler (crossing blades with a rival, in the belief that his elimination from the scene might open doors at Whitehall) had found himself hustled to the block for his pains. In my case no such strictures applied. The Queen knew naught of me—though I vowed I would remedy that fault, if this morning's exercise went my way.

While the decision rested on the hinge of fate, I let myself loll at ease. It was a trick I had long since learned, to conserve my vital forces until they exploded in action. As we rolled down the south bank I could admire the sights of Southwark, including the two fine theaters that stood there. One of these, the Rose (now almost ten years old), had made its owner a rich man. Nearby—and almost finished—stood London's finest playhouse, the Swan. Both were far more splendid than our ancient Theatre, and much larger, but the Theatre still held a warm spot in the heart of most playgoers, as the oldest and most accessible structure of its kind.

I had heard that Richard Burbage's newest temple to the drama (which he intended to call the Globe) would soon be rising in these same green fields. At the moment—it scarcely mattered that I was driving to a rendezvous with death—I let my fancy roam forward to the day when I would be actor-manager of just such a shining edifice, with poets like Master Will to fill the last seat, and a wife of my choosing to cheer me from the wings. The fact that the lady combined the sultry lure of Elvira with the demure English charms of Susanna Field was scarcely important.

A considerable crowd had gathered on the famous dueling ground. Most of them were idlers, scrapings from the under-side of any great city, who love nothing more than a behead-ing or other public circus. At each moment, I saw, barges were drifting to the landing stage on the nearby bank, to dis-charge a new freight of bespangled dandies. Here and there, to my astonishment, I noticed the presence of ladies, though these members of my audience were masked to the eyes.

The crowd swirled round our carriage as we came to a stop. A cheer went up for Raleigh, which subsided only when he lifted a hand for silence. Fitzraugh, who had been shadow-fencing to an admiring gallery of his partisans, tossed the sword to a second and gave us a mock-servile bow.

"Your servant, gentlemen. We thought you were never coming."

"We're punctual to the minute, as you well know," said Ra-leigh shortly.

"Shall we get about our business, then? The crowd's impa-tient." The dueling master took back his rapier with the words, and tossed an identical weapon in our direction. I made no move to catch it, nor did Raleigh. Instead the steel fell point down, where it struck deep in the greensward.

Fitzraugh plucked out the sword with an oath. "Doesn't your peasant offspring know how to handle fine steel?" he cried. "You've blunted the edge."

"Take back your bodkin, Fitzraugh," said Raleigh. "And stop giving yourself airs. Didn't your seconds explain *we'd* bring the blades?"

This time I caught a flash of uncertainty in the eyes of the coxcomb who faced us. But his voice still boomed for the benefit of the crowd. "Bring them on, Raleigh, and let's end this sparring with words. I've fought with every sort of blade. It's as easy to split a man with one as another."

Sir Walter nodded to Pablo, who stood behind us with the

claymores. "Call your second," he told Fitzraugh. "He must witness that the weapons are properly chosen."

My adversary's second was introduced as Master Samuel Carlton, a decent-seeming gentleman; I judged that he had been chosen to add a note of respectability to Fitzraugh's latest essay at murder. At a gesture from Raleigh, Pablo drew aside the cloths to expose the claymores. These weapons, as Susanna had remarked, were formidable indeed. The steel alone must have weighed upward of ten pounds; when they rested point down on the sod, the foot-long handles reached almost to my chin. There was but a single crossbar at the hilts, and the two-edged blades, though they lacked the sharpness of Toledo steel, were so beveled that they could split a man asunder at a single blow.

Raleigh (whose sense of showmanship was no less keen than Fitzraugh's) permitted the crowd to gape a while at the two giant cleavers. Then, as an excited buzz rose around us, he lifted both blades and extended them to my opponent. The fencing master flushed darkly.

"What jest is this?"

"You challenged my principal, giving him his choice of weapons. He chooses these."

"What in God's name are they? Some trumpery from the Theatre's lumber room?"

"Able captains have used the claymore in battle," said Raleigh sternly. "It's been my honor to oppose them—on Bally Field and elsewhere."

"No knight of the realm would touch such a bludgeon," Fitzraugh sneered.

"Master Carlton will tell you that the claymore is honored among the finest knights in Her Majesty's domain."

Carlton nodded. "The claymore is a traditional blade, Sir Harlan. Young men are still taught its use in both Scotland and Ireland."

Again Raleigh offered both swords. "Your choice, Fitzraugh," he said. "Or must this match go by default?"

The dandy snatched a blade at random, using but one hand for the act. It was an unwise gesture, for the weight of the steel all but unbalanced him, and he was forced to stagger a pace or two before he could lift it. Somewhere in the crowd a booming laugh was answered again and again, until the whole Thames-side meadow rocked with good English mirth.

For my part, I had already taken the remaining sword and twirled it above my head as though it were no heavier than a willow wand. In Ireland they say that a youth cannot call himself a man unless he can swing a claymore with either hand—although in fighting it is usually gripped in both.

As for Sir Harlan, he recovered quickly, once he had gauged the dimensions of the weapon. Watching him with a wary eye, I hoped he might be unable to heft it, but I had undervalued the sinews of a master swordsman. The cords of his neck tensed with the effort—but heft it he did, and the twirl he gave the steel was a fair imitation of my own flourish. The guffaws subsided as we faced each other. It was the inhuman silence I knew too well from the duels and hangings I had myself witnessed, the evil pleasure that each man takes in witnessing the destruction of another.

I stripped to the waist while our two seconds surveyed the dueling area. A murmur of admiration went up from the crowd when my torso was displayed; compared with the wiry frame of Sir Harlan Fitzraugh, I must have appeared massive enough—though I did not make the mistake of underestimating my opponent. He was a professional swordsman, after all, with the strength of a terrier. Now that they were accustomed to the weight of the claymore, those wrists would be like steel.

Preliminaries over, we faced each other, with the heavy broadswords point down. Fitzraugh's mouth was tight as a miser's purse. Despite his outer calm, I could guess that he seethed with rage. After all, I had just turned his well-plotted murder topsy-turvy. The size of the crowd was warning enough that our engagement had been widely heralded; since the duelist's connection with his master was well known, any humiliation visited upon him here would rebound to Essex as well.

Raleigh's face was grave as he watched from one side—and Master Carlton seemed genuinely bewildered by the turn of events. The acting president, a flint-faced captain of horse, stood between us with his saber drawn. He glanced from Fitzraugh to me. When each of us nodded in turn, he lifted his blade smartly and stepped back. It was the signal to begin.

I was balancing my sword in both hands—one on the hilt and the other supporting the blade as is customary in Ireland at the beginning of an encounter. Fitzraugh, however, gripped his weapon with both fists, as though it were a true bludgeon.

Hardly had the captain's saber fallen when he leaped forward like a monkey from his perch, hoping to catch me off guard with the first blow.

The claymore slashed down viciously in an obvious attempt to split my skull before I could defend myself. But I had only seemed to idle in my place. With a double flick of the wrists, I brought up my blade in time: the ringing crash of steel on steel echoed wildly down the riverbank. The impact shook Fitzraugh to his heels, since he had not braced himself for my maneuver.

With the first blow parried, I did not wait for the second. Swinging the broadsword in one hand, I forced my enemy to back and parry desperately, lest he be sliced in two. Not being naturally bloodthirsty, I had no real desire to dispatch him. But his vicious charge left no doubt of his intentions. I saw that I must force the battle if I were to draw first blood and thus end the duel short of a fatal outcome.

Fitzraugh was nimble as a dancer—that much I was forced to admit at once—and I realized his agility might offset my greater skill. Furthermore, since he was a born swordsman, he was learning with each thrust and parry and might well over-take me if the match was prolonged. So I continued to storm him without pause, forcing him to give ground and bringing a chorus of boos from the crowd.

Again, as he responded to this insult, the man's fierce pride was almost my undoing. Feigning a slip of the foot, he dodged beneath my next sweeping stroke as though to engage me at close quarters. For the first time I seized my claymore in both fists as his blade thrust upward, hoping to catch the steel against the hilt. But his thrust, like his apparent stumble, had been only a fraud. Even as I noted its weakness, I felt a stab of pain at my ankle as he stamped on it with an ironshod heel.

I had not expected such trickery, since this was allegedly an affair between gentlemen. When he followed his foul with a crashing thrust against my hilt, I was thrown off balance and tumbled on my back. The *code duello* demanded that he with-draw until I regained my feet—but a glance at his face as he stood with the claymore raised in both fists warned me that he would not observe the rule. The odium that would fall upon him for killing a prostrate opponent would hardly bring me back to life.

From a great distance I heard Raleigh's indignant shout, but the captain of horse, who was our supreme arbiter, made no move to stop the contest. Fitzraugh (positive that he had me at his mercy) had already reared back to deliver the death stroke. The great blade caught the sunlight as it swept downward in a hideous arc, with the finality of the headsman's ax.

I forced myself to remain immobile, to pretend that I was half stunned by the fall; only when I could measure the trajectory of the stroke did I roll aside. The claymore bit into the turf, beside my left ear. I was on my feet again before Fitzraugh could wrench it free. Gripping my own weapon in both hands and keening an Irish battle cry, I was upon him in a surge of fury that drove thought from my mind.

Twice I slashed the air in great, circling blows, forcing him to duck for his life even as he struggled to extricate his own blade. Then I stepped back deliberately, granting him a chance to defend himself. When he raised his sword again I charged him savagely, giving him no chance to strike back. This time his retreat had all the appearance of a rout. His eyes, glazed with fear when he saw I was his master, rolled imploringly toward the captain of horse, who took a tentative step forward to stop the fight.

I had no intention of permitting matters to end in a draw. Another thrust and parry gave me the opening I was seeking: darting inside his guard, I drew a long scratch down his arm, from which the blood spurted. A second thrust caught the hilt of his claymore on my point, and wrested it from his grasp, a twist I'd learned long since in Cork.

A howl of joy rose from the onlookers as his sword shot through the air, turned in a giant arc, then disappeared in the mud of the riverbank. Fitzraugh, rooted to the spot, continued to stare at me dazedly as though he fully expected me to run him through. Before he could move I reversed my sword —using it as a bodkin rather than a weapon of destruction to cut the joints that joined his doublet to his hose. The cloth ripped clean away with the stroke, exposing a lily-white backside. Again I reversed my blade, making it a paddle this time and whacking his buttocks so sharply that he sprang a good yard from the ground, like an exploding jackanapes.

The crowd was still dissolving in laughter when the captain of horse came forward. "I declare this affair ended with the drawing of first blood," he shouted. "Master MacManus is the

victor, and I charge you two gentlemen to compose your dif-
ferences and grip hands as a sign that no controversy remains
between you."

It was the standard ritual to end a duel, and he intoned it
solemnly enough—though I fancied that even his flinty face
had just escaped smiling. Leaning on my claymore (and still
puffing a bit from that final onslaught), I held out my hand to
the unbreeched popinjay who, only a moment ago, had almost
been my nemesis.

Fitzraugh stared at me dumbly as though he could not believe he was alive. Then, as the import of his defeat struck
home, his face turned white as his *derrière*. Ignoring my out-
stretched hand, he rushed to his coach without even asking his
second to accompany him. In another instant he had left the
field in a spurt of dust.

Raleigh turned to Carlton, who was gaping after the coach
—obviously unable to believe that a man of Fitzraugh's rank
could behave in so boorish a fashion.

"Are you satisfied, sir?"

The second recovered his composure. "Perfectly. May I
apologize for the behavior of my principal?"

Raleigh dismissed Fitzraugh with a gesture, as though he
were brushing aside a gnat. "We hold you no ill will for being
second to a scoundrel, Master Carlton. Will you ride back to
the city with us?"

"Thank you, no. I see friends in the crowd."

The gathering had begun to disperse, but a great number of
gentlemen (gaudy as dragonflies in their fine doublets) came
up to congratulate me before they returned to their carriages.
I will admit that I was lightheaded with compliments when Sir
Walter and I drove away at last.

For his part, he had said little while the coxcombs crowded
round me. Now that we were alone, he said nothing at all
until the coach had rolled over London Bridge again.

"That was a clever bit of swordplay, Shawn," he observed.
"Especially the final touch."

"I was carried away, sir. No gentleman would have be-
haved in such a manner."

"That's why the crowd relished it. All in all, the affair
couldn't have ended better for us both."

"Both of us?"

"But of course. Surely you noticed the size of the crowd, and the court folk who were present. That was my doing."

"I'm afraid I don't follow, sir."

"Essex planned to dispose of you—and you disposed of his bravo instead, in a manner he'll not soon forget. Before the day is out I'll have the whole story in a broadside. One way or another it's bound to reach the Queen's ear. When it does, you can breathe easier. Elizabeth had her crotchets—but she's a champion of fair play and she enjoys a joke. If we handle our cards properly, Essex won't dare to molest you further." He paused and put his hand on my arm in a gesture of apology. "Forgive me, Shawn, if I'm making you seem too much a puppet——"

"Don't think I mind that," I said.

"I'm advancing my fortune, lad, and I'm using you as the tool. But you've no cause for complaint. Your own career is being helped as well."

That much I could see clearly enough. Had it not been for my original resemblance to Raleigh, I would not be sitting in his coach today. Nor would I have found my name on every tongue in London after my first appearance at the Theatre. Finally, I had grasped the fact that this duel (which had seemed so desperate a gamble) could open still other doors— if I would trust Sir Walter to provide the key.

"Please go on," I begged.

"There's little more to be said, my boy. Once the Queen has heard of you, I'll have Cecil present you at a levee."

"It's more than I dared dream of, sir——" I broke off on that, realizing that I had not spoken the truth. "I *did* hope that I might some day meet the Queen," I admitted. "But not that it would happen so soon."

"In this case, time is all-important. Once she's seen you and remarked your resemblance to me, the game's over, so far as Essex is concerned; if a hair of your head is touched, she'll know just who is to blame. No one in England dare harm a man she fancies—as some have learned to their sorrow."

"What if she takes no notice of me?"

Raleigh smiled, even as his eyes clouded. It was a look I had already noticed, when his mind turned back to the past.

"She'll notice you—I'll give odds on that."

I felt a sudden shiver of dread while he continued to plan aloud, as though he were but half aware of my presence. Already it was apparent that he hoped the sight of me would stir the woman who had once loved him so madly. Did he expect me to pick up the romance where he had lost it? Was I to give a woman of sixty-odd the illusion that springtime had returned to her life—perhaps even to her boudoir?

"Do you expect me to advance your voyage to the New World?" I asked.

His fingers fastened on my arm. "That's what I'm asking, lad. I'm sure you have wit enough to manage it."

"I'll try, sir," I said, glad that I was seated. Had I been on my feet, I knew my knees would be quaking. "If the occasion arises, that is——"

"You'll have your chance, Shawn. Leave that to Gossip's tongue, and Sir Robert Cecil."

With those words, he settled in his corner. Grotesque though the thought was, I felt he envied me.

"Most of us would sell our souls to be twenty again," he said. "Through a twist of fate, I've been granted that boon. Let's not be cowards, Shawn: let's make the most of it."

CHAPTER VIII

Tomcat's Night Out

GOSSIP, as Raleigh had suggested, has its own wings.

At the afternoon's performance, when I strode on stage in my uniform as captain of the guard, I was ready for the roar of applause that greeted me.

That morning, when he left me at the stage alley, I had not entered the Theatre at once. Instead I had wandered at random on Finsbury Fields (with the faithful Pablo at my heels) while my mind struggled to encompass the prospects that opened before me. I will confess that my feelings were mixed as I reflected on the part I would play in my mentor's destiny: no honest Irishman could face the thought of entering the court of the Virgin Queen without a *frisson* of pure animal terror. At the same time, the thought had a special, tingling excitement. My heart was swelling with pride when I returned to the sewing room at last, with only a moment left to don my costume.

Susanna was much occupied when I appeared—so busy, in fact, that she took no notice of me whatever after she had scolded me for my tardiness. But I was positive that the news of my feat in Southwark had already reached her ears. Knowing just what favor I would be asking of her tonight (and guessing what her reply would be), I was still oddly reluctant to put my new-minted charm to the test when the performance ended. Instead of cornering her—as was my custom— I sought out Master Will instead.

At the moment I needed a confidant badly. Wisely or not, I found myself telling him the story of the duel and Raleigh's plans for me at court.

"You're rarely fortunate, Shawn," he said. "With Sir Walter to advise you, there's no telling where you'll end—providing you keep your head, and your strength."

"What if this business involves me with the Queen?"

"Don't play the bumpkin forever. Raleigh made his fortune between the royal sheets. Perhaps you'll do likewise."

"She was younger then."

"What's youth to do with passion? Our Queen will be riggish until death claims her. If you're offered the chance to leap into her bed, shut your eyes if you must, but leap all the same."

"I'm not sure I'd have the courage."

Master Will continued to study me with a detachment I could hardly resent. It was as though my life was a plot too baffling for even a master dramatist to solve. "If your conscience restrains you," he said, "still its nagging. Remember, this is for England's glory."

"How so?"

"Let's assume you please the Queen; let's say she gives you the command to love, and you obey. Later, out of gratitude for your prowess, let's say she grants Raleigh a patent to invade the New World." The playwright rumbled with laughter as he slapped my shoulder. "Chin up, lad! Can't you see your act might change the course of history?"

I shrugged off his sophistry. "What if I'm in love with someone else?"

"She'll wait—if she observes you're en route to fame and riches."

"I'm not too sure of that."

"Take my word for it, they usually do. A chance like this will never come to you again. There is a tide in the affairs of men, Which, taken at the flood, leads on to fortune——"

"Stop quoting your own lines!" I admonished him tartly.

Shakespeare accepted my rebuke with a good-natured grin. "When your testing comes, you'll see how right I am. There's a brain between those big ears—though it's a bit sluggish at times." He left me on that, with his odd, almost strutting walk, his head cocked at the same insolent angle. The echo of his laughter lingered.

It was only when I stood alone on the empty stage (and stared up at the first stars in the circle of sky above the pit) that the import of my reluctance to embrace a royal opportunity struck home. Was it possible that I was in love—with Susanna Field?

I had always fought shy of love, as young men will. Such knowing bedmates as Elvira Quesada had kept my passions healthy and left me fancy-free. How could I surrender my heart to Puss, who had given me no more than a teasing kiss or two, and the garter that still nested in my doublet? How (when I ticked off the long list of wenches I had bedded) could I make man's deepest surrender to a wispy lass I'd mistaken for a fresh-cheeked boy?

Only that morning I'd decided to seduce her at the first convenient moment; virgin or no, I'd expected my assault to succeed. Tonight, with my prize in my grasp, I continued to stand irresolute. With England's great on my side, with the Golden Ones of Manoa beckoning, would I turn mooncalf and lose freedom along with fortune?

A sixth sense urged me to flee the Theatre while there was time for flight. A small voice within me insisted that this could be greater peril than Essex's bravos. Yet my stubborn male pride continued to mutter that no woman under heaven could turn me from my purpose.

Susanna was in the sewing room. As I had hoped, she was alone, fitting a lining to a cloak by the light of a rush lamp. When she heard my step, she lifted her eyes from her work, and gave me her most mocking grimace.

"Behold, the handsome knight returns unscarred," she said —declaiming the words as though she were reciting blank verse. "Why does he walk so warily tonight?"

The mockery piqued me; I had half expected her to run to me in tears, as we rejoiced together over my victory. "Would you have liked it better had I returned on my shield?"

"Spare me the story of your encounter," she said. "I've heard it ten times over."

"Did you hear that Fitzraugh almost killed me?"

"I don't believe that for a moment. You're indestructible—like your self-esteem."

"Then it scarce matters to you if I live or die?"

"I didn't say *that*, Shawn MacManus——"

"You didn't dare. Else why would you give me your favor before the duel?" I produced the garter with a flourish and pretended to lift her petticoats and restore it to its place.

Even in the feeble glow of the lamp, I saw that she had colored as she snatched her skirt away, though her manner was peckish as ever. "Very well," she said. "I'm glad fate spared you—since you're beginning to be useful here. Or were, until you began hobnobbing with the great."

The rancor in her tone gave me a clue to her mood. "Is it my fault that Raleigh befriends me? Would you have me refuse his favors?"

"By no means," she said in a softer voice. "But no man can inhabit two worlds, Shawn."

"I'll always be part of *this* world——"

"The Theatre?"

"Because it's your world too—and the only real home I've known."

"You'll sing a different tune, once Raleigh has made you as great a nabob as himself."

"We both belong here, Puss," I told her. "Just as we'll belong in that new playhouse Dick Burbage plans to build across the Thames. Even if I cross the sea with Raleigh I'll return to the Globe—and to you."

"Don't think I'll faint for joy at that avowal. Even if you meant it."

"I'll prove I mean it—by taking whatever chance Raleigh offers me. When I've grown rich under his protection I'll buy a share of the Globe. It's as simple as that. Why won't you believe me?"

"Why not reach for the moon while you're about it?" But the tartness had gone from her voice, and her eyes were soft in the half-light. After all, my vision was close to her own heart; she could hardly fail to see it clearly.

Her garter was still in my palm. I offered it gently, but made no move to touch her.

"Answer one question truly," I said. "Why did you give me this?"

"To bring you luck, of course."

"May I put it on, as you promised?"

"I made no such promise; I said only that we'd discuss it——"

"Shall we discuss it now?"

She did not stir while I moved forward slowly, turned back one petticoat and then another, then slipped the windblown flower into place above her knee. Wise in this ancient game, I did not venture further. Instead, I slipped an arm about her waist and turned her lips to mine.

This time it was no feather-soft kiss she gave me, but a lingering buss that sent my senses rocking. Then her own arms were about my neck, and I was lost forevermore in her sweetness, drowned in desires that teased me out of thought. While the spell lasted Shawn MacManus ceased to exist: a brand-new lad had replaced the apish libertine. If this be love, I thought, it's finer than every stolen passion of this earth.

"Shawn dear——"

"Yes, sweet?"

"I never knew it was like this—I never *dreamed*——"

"Nor did I."

My head cleared with that grave avowal, and I found the will to put her from me. "Now we've made that discovery," I said, "I'll bid you good night, Puss."

"Good night?"

"We'll meet again tomorrow." The words were half a mutter, but I knew that I had escaped in time, that she scarce understood the passions that had brought her so close to surrender.

"You're a strange wooer, Master Irishman," she whispered.

"So I am. You'll thank me someday—for that strangeness."

"Must you go so soon?"

"I've an engagement in Shoreditch—I can't postpone it."

My exit was a lame one indeed, but it took me from the sewing room and into the fresh winter night of the stage alley.

Pablo emerged from the shadows—a copper-dark ghost, whose schedule never varied.

"I was about to seek you out, señor," he said quietly.

"Tonight I'll need no bodyguard."

"Sir Walter ordered me to follow you—even when you go visiting."

"Who said anything about visiting?"

"Enrique is here, señor—the Quesada coachman."

"Enrique?"

"Señorita Moreno y Quesada sent him. He's to drive you into London."

Hours later, in the first light of morning, I wakened in the great, curtained tent of yet another strange bed, as Elvira's questing lips sought mine. Even in the gloom, there was a pearly glow about her, as though the lusts we had slaked through a long night had given her flesh a special radiance.

"Kiss me again, light of my soul," she whispered. "Never stop kissing me——"

Later she lay back in her nest of pillows and watched with sleepy contentment while I threw her windows wide to the promise of sunrise. Below, the Thames gleamed like a great coiled snake as the last star winked out.

"Stay a moment more, Shawn. Talk to me."

"What of your uncle?"

"I told you the old fool is in Oxford."

There was a decanter on the night table. I poured a glass for each of us before seating myself on the bed. Even with all passion spent, I could not help admiring the picture she made at that moment.

"Tell me, *querido*," she said, as she sipped the wine, "what did Don Pedro ask of you, when you visited him in the *sala?*"

"He seemed pleased that I was established in London."

"You're content with your work at the Theatre?"

"At the moment acting is only a toy," I said. "I'm waiting for word from Raleigh."

"All London knows you've joined forces—and suspects why."

I took the plunge, since I could do no less. "He's offered me a commission on his flagship when he makes his next voyage to Virginia."

"When do you leave?"

"Only the Queen knows that answer. Raleigh can't stir until she grants him a patent."

"At least I can rejoice you aren't sailing tomorrow," she said.

"What of your own plans, Elvira? Isn't it true that you, too, plan a voyage to the New World?"

Her lazy eyelids fluttered. "Who told you that?"

"I know you're niece to the governor of Trinidad. You can hardly blame me for making inquiries."

"You're right, Shawn. Don Pedro isn't my only protector. You might even say that I'm in London on sufferance. The governor takes it ill that I should live thus, without so much as a duenna to guard me——"

"From men like myself?"

"From the manifold temptations of the world," she said. "Fie on you, *Irlandés,* for reminding a girl that she's an unrepentant sinner."

"I'd never reproach you for so sweet a sin," I said. "How is this Trinidad uncle called?"

"His name is Don Antonio de Berreo. We are blood relations: the Quesadas are tied to the Mornos only by marriage."

Ignorant as I was of the proliferations of a Spanish family tree, I suspected that this statement was a lie. If Elvira's departure for Trinidad was imminent, it was far more likely that she would serve as Quesada's messenger.

"We may sail at the same time," I told her. "Raleigh plans to leave in the new year if he obtains his patent."

"Could you be mistaken as to his objective?"

I shook my head. "Only yesterday he showed me the log of the colonizing voyage he sent out to Virginia."

"The one wiped out by the aborigines?"

"The same," I said—not too surprised at her knowledge of that ill-starred expedition. "He means to try again, on the same spot, with a larger force."

"Virginia is within the Spanish domains, Shawn; he's no right to trespass."

"I can't believe that your King sets much store by the area. What has he done to hold it—besides keeping a garrison at St. Augustine?"

"Did Raleigh tell you this, *chiquito?*"

"Almost word for word."

I watched her stretch her whole body in a long, lazy yawn —as though my glib answers had removed some inner tension. "I know only what Don Pedro says of these matters," she told me. "He, too, does not think the land called Virginia has much value."

"The new world is vast, Elvira. If the English keep to the north, there should be living room for all."

"I trust you're right," she said. "In all events, let's pray we're granted a few more weeks in London." She leaned forward and kissed me warmly. "Now you must really go: I can hear the larks in the garden."

"It is a nightingale, and not the lark."

"Are you a poet too? Your Master Will could not have penned a finer line."

"The line does belong to Shakespeare," I admitted. "It's from a tragedy he's writing now——"

"With death for the lovers?"

"Death in a tomb. We've begged for a happier ending—but it's hard to change a poet's tune."

"Let's hope *our* story has a better finish."

"Why shouldn't it, *alma de mi corazón?*" I asked carefully.

"That's for you to decide, Shawn MacManus."

"In what way?"

"As you've just guessed, I'll be joining my uncle in Trinidad before long. Would you follow me there, if I provided the reason?"

"Desert Raleigh, you mean?"

"What if he's been deceiving you—and this story of a voyage to Virginia is a blind? Some say he's planning to go in search of El Dorado."

With each word she spoke I could feel the pressure on my wits increase. Then, to my infinite relief, she broke into a laugh and reached up to tousle my hair before drawing my head down to the fragrant pillow of her breast. For a moment (while I pretended to rest there in ecstatic content) I had the fearful sensation of falling into a pit from which there was no escaping.

"Don't look so puzzled, *Irlandés,*" she said. "If Raleigh is hoodwinking the public, *you* aren't aware of it."

I held my tongue, recalling my mentor's own words when he first took me into his confidence. Elvira would never be-

lieve me if I said that it was the Queen's privilege—not ours
—to choose the objective of our proposed voyage.

"Raleigh's star rises and sets in Virginia," I protested at
last. "I'm convinced of that."

"Is Virginia your guiding star as well?"

"Only because it's the short road to fortune."

She let me go with that last avowal, after I had finished my
dressing and kissed her one more time. I quitted her bed-
chamber with what grace I could muster. Despite my narrow
escape, I felt that I had acquitted myself passably—and could
only pray that Quesada would believe her report.

It was full morning when the coach creaked into Shoreditch
Road. I had hoped to slip into the Theatre quietly and catch
forty winks on my pallet before the long chore of setting the
stage began. To my chagrin, I found the back door locked
and was forced to knock long and lustily before a key turned
within. Susanna admitted me, a kerchief knotted round her
curls and a skillet in her hand. From the quarters she shared
with her father came the odor of frying meat. The girl herself, despite the dressing sack she wore, seemed fresh as the
morning—and almost buoyantly unconcerned at my low-
voiced greeting.

"Come in, Master Irishman," she said. "You needn't look
so bashful."

Try as I might, I could not meet her eyes, while she continued to study me with a coolness far more wounding than
anger or contempt. Too late, I realized that her kitchen
looked down on Shoreditch Road; she must have heard the
coach lumber up—and recognized it as Quesada's.

"Did I disturb you, Puss? I'm sorry——"

"Think nothing of it," she said airily. "I'm always up at this
hour, to let in the tomcats."

CHAPTER IX

A Levee at Whitehall

AFTER my encounter with Fitzraugh I had fully expected life to continue at the same dizzy pace. Actually, in the weeks that followed, my round of days was humdrum enough, though I will admit that I was kept almost too busy to think.

Now that the English winter had begun, and the threat of plague (always at its worst in the hot months) had receded from London, business at the various theaters was booming. Master Burbage's playhouse, as always, set the pace for the others. Besides the extensive repertoire, Shakespeare was readying two new plays. One of them was a knockabout farce which he called *The Comedy of Errors,* whose plot eludes me today. Another was the tragedy from which I had quoted a line at Quesada's; it was called *Romeo and Juliet,* and dealt with the trials of two young lovers of noble, but bitterly hostile, Italian families.

In addition to my duties as a scene shifter and general factotum in the backstage area, I was given a part in the latter production. The fellow I played was named Tybalt, and a black villain he was, stirring enmity on all sides and muttering curses in his beard until he was laid low by Romeo's sword. As for Susanna, she was permitted to understudy the heroine. Occasionally, when the spindle-shanked boy who played the part was absent, Susanna read the part at rehearsal, so beautifully that I was not ashamed to weep as I listened from the wings.

The tragedy was as yet unready for the boards (Master Will was a great reviser, and not above borrowing ideas from anyone in shouting distance when a rehearsal was simmering). Burbage proposed to give it for the first time in the spring. What occupied us at the moment was the polishing of that droll mishmash of nonsense, *The Comedy of Errors*. This play had already been commissioned for a command performance at court, in the palace the Queen maintained at Greenwich, a smallish town not too far down-river from London.

Meanwhile the usual schedule of performances had continued in Shoreditch, and I had been privileged to rant my way through a series of roles. Susanna's path crossed mine constantly—and now and again I tried (halfheartedly it is true) to pick up our old camaraderie. It would have been easier if she had railed at me outright, or even teased me with the waspish wit she had used in my apprentice days. By this time, however, I had learned my lines passably and made myself useful in a dozen ways. The hardest taskmaster would have found little to scold—and Susanna, I admit to my sorrow, seemed at times all but oblivious of my presence.

On occasions when my blood was up, I could tell myself that this attitude was only a self-defensive one, which I could have broken with a word. At others I felt that I had lost her even as I found her, that my return from Elvira's bed (only a few hours after my avowals in the sewing room) had been a transgression that nothing could repair. To make matters worse, Elvira continued insatiable in her demands, with the result that the coach frequently awaited me at the stage alley, to return me there in yet another dawn.

Such was the state of affairs when Quesada himself summoned me for an accounting. I told him the same story I had been repeating behind the curtains of his niece's bed. Perhaps it was only his way of testing my honesty. In all events, it seemed that I dissembled enough, for I left his house with a heavy purse. He promised me another if I could warn him when the die was cast and Raleigh's departure an actuality.

As for Raleigh, he was at Durham House but little during these weeks, occupied as he was with the outfitting of his flotilla and the recruitment of prospective colonists. Our only communication was a brief note. He enclosed the proof of the broadside he had ordered composed in my honor and advised me that he would send me word when the time was ripe for my audience with the Queen.

The sheet was typical of its kind. Though it was unsigned, I was told at the Theatre that it had been composed by Master

Thomas Green, the best practitioner of this curious trade in London. As was the custom, it was written mainly in verse— or rather, in doggerel couplets. From first to last, of course, its aim was to ridicule both Fitzraugh and Essex. To this end, it was mainly a running account of the duel, which left no doubt of the identity of the opponents though the writer was careful to avoid our actual names.

Under the title *How David Bested Goliath*, the story began with characteristic impudence, in a prose poetry that can only be described as atrocious:

> *Come listen, lords and ladies all,*
> *To my tale of a courtly Goliath's fall,*
> *A knightly bravo whose death-dealing skill*
> *Had forced all opponents to bow to his will,*
> *Till an Irish David with English kin*
> *Gave his Scottish claymore a fearful spin*
> *And, matching the bravo blow for blow,*
> *Disarmed him with ease, and laid him low.*
> *Then, sparing his life, tore his breeches aside*
> *And warmed with steel his naked backside....*

There was more in the same vein. The story ended with the following couplets:

> *Now such a brave victory by this Irish gallant*
> *Must needs show the Queen his peculiar talent.*
> *For he bested a bully at a game all his own*
> *And discomfited someone quite close to the throne.*
> *The fair sex must ***** condemn as a cad*
> *Who sent his paid swordsman to kill this fair lad,*
> *For servant's deeds master's needs always show true*
> *And this deed Lord ***** will forever rue.*

A few days after I received Raleigh's note, the broadside was hawked outside the Theatre. By nightfall it was the conversation piece of every tavern in London.

For a time, I felt sure that Essex would find some way to avenge the insult. But it seemed that Milord was walking warily now, for there were no further attacks on my person. Nor was the hoped-for summons from Whitehall forthcoming, though I started at each knock in the days that followed, positive that it was Elizabeth's equerry, come in person to greet me.

As I have implied, my expectation of an audience with the Queen had almost entirely subsided when word reached me that Raleigh was at Durham House again and wished to see me there at once. I found him pacing his study, with a tailor in attendance. In the next hour I was fitted for my first court costume and given careful instruction on how to comport myself. Lord Cecil, it seemed, had arranged for my informal appearance at the last outdoor levee of the year, when he would introduce me to the Queen in passing, as it were, confident by now that word of my doings in London had reached her ear.

The delay, I gathered, had been deliberate. It was partly to give Essex a chance to stew in his own juice, and partly to allow the gossip to grow among Elizabeth's retinue, most of whom had now taken the opportunity to see me perform at the Theatre.

The costume that Raleigh had chosen for my great moment showed his flair for the dramatic. Left to myself, I would have arrayed myself as gaudily as a peacock. Sir Walter had decided to underplay, with clothing that was subdued enough to suit the current tastes, yet cut so artfully that each line made the most of my physique, whose good points I need stress no further.

My trunk hose were of deepest black; over these I wore knee-high cordovan boots, as soft as any actor's buskin. My doublet was dark blue, the puffed sleeves slashed with crimson and azure, and my ruff of the purest white. For headgear, I was given a velvet cap with a white crane's feather, needing no raised crown to give me added height. My cloak was dark, with a crimson-and-azure lining to match the puffs of my sleeves.

I wore no weapon but the small, heavily jeweled dagger then in fashion for a levee—and, since I had not yet adopted the English beard (the actor must remain clean-shaven), my cheek and jowl remained smooth as any boy's.

Raleigh sat at his worktable while his valet dressed me. When the last button was in place he waved the man from the room and reached for his inevitable pipe with a sigh that was more than a little rueful.

"Myself at twenty, by Our Lady!"

"Let's hope I'm worthy of the comparison, sir," I said—and

my voice betrayed the fact that I was quaking in my boots at the thought of glimpsing my first queen. Raleigh must have sensed my fears, for he gave me a smart cuff behind the ear.

"Head up, Shawn," he said. "Chin out—and damn anyone who doesn't say you're an uncommon fine fellow."

"*Anyone?*"

"The Queen will endorse my judgment. Have no fear of that. Just walk easily and tell yourself you were born to the purple; your blarney will do the rest."

"God grant you're right, sir."

"You *are* quite comfortable, I trust?"

"This doublet seems tight across the shoulders."

"I ordered it that way," he said, and grinned at me around the pipe. "You see, lad, if you were an ordinary popinjay, I'd have puffed the fabric to disguise a puny shoulder. With the doublet cut tight, the Queen need not guess what sort of man's underneath, even if it's true that her eyesight is fading."

Lord Cecil's coach arrived in another moment. I walked out with my best stride, trying to imitate the easy yet arrogant gait that was Sir Walter's hallmark. There is a saying that clothes make the man; I saw its proof that afternoon, when Milord's lackeys jumped to open the coach door, with as much bowing and scraping as they would have offered a prince.

Cecil (resplendent in canary-yellow hose and jade-green doublet, with his medals proudly displayed at the left breast) received me with the grave courtesy one accords an equal. On the short drive to Whitehall he chatted constantly on various topics of the day, without asking for more than a few words of response. Knowing that he was putting me at my ease, I settled in my corner of the equipage and did my utmost to calm the race of my pulses.

I could have wished that Raleigh had presented me, but his appearances at court these days were rare, and the sight of us, side by side, might have done his cause more harm than good. I knew I could rely on Sir Robert for the informal touch so vital in such moments. Certainly I was no trespasser among my betters, but a man with a mission vital to England's future.

Since today's levee was an outdoor affair, we did not approach the palace by its main gate. Instead we turned to a smaller entrance, where a long, narrow alley opened to a greensward prodigal with fancifully cut boxwoods and swarming with courtiers of every stripe. Most of these coxcombs seemed to be talking at once, and the air was strident with their gabble. Wine was passing on a score of trays, as spindle-shanked lackeys bustled at furious speed to satisfy a collective thirst that seemed insatiable.

The women (I counted them by the dozens, though they were far outnumbered by the men) seemed to enjoy their tipple, but I saw few outward signs of drunkenness among either sex; Elizabeth Tudor's perceptions had not dimmed with age —and a slip of the tongue in her presence (whatever the cause) could have dire aftermaths.

In all honesty I will admit a certain disappointment at my first view of the gathering. The picture I had formed in my mind was rather more colorful than the reality. I had, in fact, visioned a sunburst of pageantry more splendid than the treasures of Cathay. Save for the contending voices, the court of Elizabeth was on the sober side. Most of the men were in dress as severely dark as my own. The women (for all the daring show of bosom in gowns cut to the wishbone) had been careful not to outshine their sovereign. Here and there —as in Cecil's case—a dandy strutted in colors that would have shamed the rainbow; I could not help but wonder if these were the Queen's favorites who thus advertised their perquisites.

There was no sign of Essex in the gathering, and for this I could be grateful. I caught a glimpse of Sir Roger Williams. He cocked an eyebrow at the sight of me, then bowed, for all the world as though he had not plotted my death the first time he saw me. I nodded courteously, though I would rather have put his neck within my grasp.

The lawn sloped to join the river, and it was here that the press was thickest, around the open marquee where the Queen was holding court. My heart rose to my throat when my eyes found her at last (thanks to my height, I could see over the plumes of the men who swarmed around her). Today she sat on a dais, in a throne-chair draped with a cloth of gold. The tiara she wore blazed no more brightly than her red hair (the gossips insisted that she had dyed it thus for thirty years), and the thrust of her fine Tudor nose, even at that distance, suggested the prow of a ship under full sail.

I knew she was in her sixties—yet she would have stood out

In any gathering, even without her jewels, the emerald-crusted mace in her left fist, and the flaring, high-ruffed gown of shocking green, heavy with an embroidery of pearls. Now that I was in her actual presence, I doubted if she had ever been beautiful. But she was still a handsome woman, though the paints and pomades that stiffened her cheeks made her seem almost an effigy of herself until one noticed the flashing eyes.

So much I gathered as my faltering steps approached the outdoor throne: if the levee itself had fallen below my expectations, its core and center seemed far more vital than my most sanguine dreams. Even as Sir Robert Cecil began to elbow his way through the press that surrounded Elizabeth, I had no real notion how to comport myself. In Raleigh's interest it was imperative that I catch the Queen's ear and eye. I said a short prayer to my patron saint and lifted my chin as I had been instructed.

At least I could tell myself that Shawn MacManus was the equal of any bright-feathered vulture on this lawn—and the superior of most. Ignoring the murmurs that followed us, and the fox-eyed glances that remarked my resemblance to Sir Walter, I felt my mental muscles harden for my task, even as my biceps had knotted to beat down Fitzraugh.

Sir Robert laid a warning hand on my arm as the Queen's glance found me. I saw her eyes widen in genuine interest as she gave me a stare that seemed to burn the clothes from my body. Etiquette demanded that we keep our place until we were noticed by the chamberlain who stood just behind the throne-chair—or the Queen herself should address us. In this case, as I had hoped, we received the latter summons.

"Come near me, sweet Cecil," she cried, and the voice that issued from that painted mouth was lusty as a girl's, for all its cracked timbre.

Sir Robert approached the throne and bowed, a movement which I duplicated. Richard Burbage had schooled me in the court bow until I was passably adept. I watched Sir Robert's leg, and when I saw him tense it to rise, I did likewise. When I raised my head I was eye to eye with England's Queen—and found her stare no less intense at close quarters. It was outright hypnotism; while it lasted I was but dimly aware of my surroundings. All that remained were those fiery eyes.

Sir Robert's voice seemed to reach me from a vast distance,

though he was at my elbow. "Your Majesty, may I present Master Shawn MacManus?"

I offered the throne a second bow, without removing my gaze from its occupant. The hypnosis ceased as abruptly as though Elizabeth Tudor had dropped a shutter inside her brain. When she offered me a hand to kiss (the courtiers buzzed like angry bees at the honor) I felt no sense of strain. Whatever the power she possessed over men, she had suspended it to put me at my ease. Already she seemed only a sharp-eyed old woman who deserved my courtesy and respect.

"Welcome to our presence, Master Shawn MacManus," she said, in that odd, cracked voice which still vibrated with a lust for living. "What's this I hear—and read—of the quarrels you've been picking with the gentlemen of my court?"

I was still bowed above her hand. In sober truth, I was searching a spot to kiss, among her thronging rings. "I fear Your Majesty has been misinformed," I said, and heard another buzz of comment as the court leaned forward and seemed to listen with a single avid ear.

"So?" The gimlet gaze was boring into my soul again, but I held my ground, with all the resolution I could muster. "And what is *your* version, lad?"

"First-off, ma'am," I said, "I picked no quarrel. Secondly, the affair has been settled to my satisfaction. It would be ungentlemanly to speak of my opponent now."

Again I heard the drone of tongues; remembering the rages for which she was famous, I wondered if I had been too forward. Still, if I'd judged Elizabeth aright, she was one to respect spirit in a man and had a sense of fairness as well.

"Spoken like a courtier—and an Irishman," she said. "Do they often grow them as handsome in that country?"

"All Irishmen are handsome, ma'am," I said boldly. "The difference lies merely in your point of view."

She laughed for the first time at my sally, and her merriment was as deep-throated as a man's. Elizabeth had always loved a jest, no matter how near the knuckle it might be. "By all the gods, Cecil," she cried, " 'tis a forward rogue you've brought to us today. Are you loyal to me, Master Irishman?"

"Your Majesty has but to test the temper of my devotion."

"And to England?"

I dared to match the painted grin. "To Your Majesty first

and always. Afterward to the land of my nativity. Then to England."

"By God, fellow, you've a cutting edge to your tongue," she shouted. "We find him refreshing, Cecil. You must bring him to us again."

"Of course, Your Majesty," murmured Sir Robert—and I needed no second glance to realize from her change of address that my brief interview was over. Again in unison, we offered the throne a final bow and backed from its presence, until the swirling crowd of sycophants hid the Queen from view. With the gentle pressure of an elbow, Sir Robert guided me to a spot out of earshot of the staring groups.

"You acquitted yourself well, Master Shawn," he said. "Well enough, in fact, to deserve an encore, as they say in your trade."

His praise was the very medicine I needed; now that my ordeal was over, I had gone cold to the finger ends. "D'you think Sir Walter will be pleased?"

"Rest assured of that. You could not have served him better." He lifted a goblet from a passing tray and gave it to me with a smile. "Unlimber, lad," he advised, as I drained the wine in a swallow. "Queens are mortal, like other women; 'tis only legend that assumes they're divine."

"I'm happy I didn't disgrace you, Sir Robert."

"Far from it, as I told you. I've some people I must see privately, now we've paid our respects. Can you find entertainment for yourself until I return?"

"Just being here is entertainment enough," I told him heartily. Not that I was altogether at ease when he left me. I had already observed that Sir Roger Williams was watching me from the partial ambush of a boxwood. I had expected him to pounce on me—and braced for his approach.

"Today, Master MacManus, you seem uncommon fond of yourself," the soldier said. "Perhaps you've good cause."

"You're a cool un, Sir Roger," I said. "I'm surprised you've the gall to face me."

He accepted the thrust with aplomb. "Believe me, it is not my custom to send two men to waylay another."

"But you sent them nonetheless."

"So I did. It's a soldier's business to obey orders. I'll wager your appearance here today is not of your own planning."

"Sir Walter Raleigh has taken me into his employ," I said stiffly. "Naturally I serve his interests as best I can."

"Raleigh is smart as they come," he acknowledged. "This time he's excelled himself. You'll admit we did our best to stop you both?"

"Your very best."

" 'Twas wise of you to force yourself upon him promptly, Master Shawn."

"You're wrong there. I did nothing of the kind."

"Have it your way. The mere fact of the resemblance made it inevitable you should meet—if you lived so long. Unfortunately for us, you've managed to do just that."

"No thanks to you, Sir Roger—or to Milord Essex."

"And you've no love for me, as a consequence. I can't blame you for that. More's the pity, for I liked the cut of your jaw when I first saw you at the Theatre."

I shrugged off the compliment. There was no answer I could rightly make, though I did half believe him.

"Fate has made us enemies," he said. "There's no going back. Still—to even the game—I'll warn you not to push too far."

"What does that mean?"

Sir Roger glanced carelessly down the velvet-green lawn, to the crowd that still elbowed for space inside the marquee. "The old girl's still hotter than most wenches in their teens," he said. "Catch her fancy and you'll probably find yourself in her bed. You might even become a man of parts in court."

"Like your patron?"

" 'Tis conceivable—again, providing you live that long. Of course, now you've had your spot of glory, you might still return to Cork. The Queen's in need of bailiffs there; you could amass a fortune in a hurry."

"Is that a bribe to leave England?"

"Hardly, Master Shawn. I'm only a simple man of Mars, with nothing to offer anyone."

"But Essex would make it possible?"

"Who mentioned Milord's name? We were conducting a discussion of what might be—a practice your countrymen are said to love."

I found myself joining in his chuckle. He was bold as a brass monkey, but I could hardly help liking him. "Tell your patron it's too late to drive me out of England," I said. "It's also much too late to order my assassination. Remember, the Queen has seen me."

Williams rubbed his chin. "You've a point there."

"Tell Milord Essex one thing more, while you're about it," I said. "He's aware I'm to do what I can to help Sir Walter secure his patent. Tell him to keep clear of me while I achieve that end—and I'll do nothing to spoil his own prospects."

"It's a bargain, lad," he told me gravely, but with a glint of humor in his eyes.

"See you keep it, Sir Roger," I said, and left him with a brisk salute, since I was already in search of other quarry. While we talked I had noticed a familiar, raven-haired figure on the edge of the crowd, with her hand tucked through a young officer's arm. Now that I'd given Williams a piece of my mind, it seemed good policy to deflect Elvira Quesada from her escort.

It took some little persuasion to dismiss her gallant—who insisted that her uncle had put the defenseless girl under his protection. He was introduced to me as Captain Felipe de Vera, a military aide to the embassy; I found him a snobbish braggart whom it would have given me great pleasure to thrash on the spot. Not that I was overeager to be seen alone with Elvira at this time, but it was evident from her first sign of recognition that she had tidings to impart.

When her blue-blooded escort had gone his way at last (with his waxed mustachios still pointed skyward in disdain), the minx teased me a bit longer before she imparted her secret.

"It was my good fortune to find you here, Shawn," she whispered as she steered me skillfully to a pavilion at the water's edge, one of those gilt-and-gingerbread gazebos that are built especially for a *scène à deux*. "Tío Pedro will be at home tonight. I dared not send for you——"

"Then this meeting is indeed inspired." Although I was holding her hand under the ambush of my cloak, I dared not kiss it openly, with so many eyes upon us. "Tell me your wishes. I'll see that they are obeyed instantly."

"I hope that you mean that, *querido*——"

"Do you doubt my devotion?"

"Not for a moment. But you *did* swear that you'd see my wishes were obeyed."

"Say the word," I begged. "I'll slip in by the postern tonight
—and a pox on your uncle."

"Would you board ship with me next month, and sail for
Trinidad?"

Braced though I was for a suggestion of this sort, it still
came as a shock. "Would Don Antonio de Berreo welcome a
wild Irishman in Trinidad?"

"He could employ you as a go-between if danger should
threaten from the English. Believe me, you'd be useful in
many ways."

"I fear your uncle won't share your views."

"I have his promise to offer you employment—if you'll accept it. The letter came this morning."

"You've written to the New World in my behalf?"

"Believe me, I can advance your fortunes ten times faster
than Raleigh."

"May I ask *when* you wrote De Berreo?"

"After our first night at the Swan and Dolphin."

You *are* a sly baggage, I thought—and wondered, for a
moment of panic, if she was lying. There was something
about her manner this afternoon that suggested the contrary.
Was it possible that she had begun this game on Quesada's
orders and ended by desiring me for myself alone?

"You've sworn in two languages that you love me," she
said. "Was it no more than the desire that goes with the
dawn?"

"Soul of my heart, you know better——"

"We'll leave England together, then?"

"How can we—when I've promised to sail with Raleigh? A
man of honor must keep his word."

The answer seemed to satisfy her, for the nonce. "I know
it's wrong of me to interfere in your affairs. But I felt I must
speak. I'm not a free agent, you know. Few women are in
Spain—regardless of their station."

"There's no way you can remain in England?"

"What does England mean to me, with you away?"

"I'll return in time, Elvira. I promise that. Now that I've
the right to ask you to wait." Our love scene, I felt, was getting out of hand. In her boudoir I had always smothered such
arguments in kisses—but that was clearly impractical here.

"Perhaps I won't wait," she said, with a toss of her head.

"Would it interest you to know that De Vera aspires to be my *novio*? We sail for Trinidad on the same ship."

The Spanish dandy, I recalled, had a shifty eye, for all his warlike manner. I had already surmised that he would prove an indifferent performer, on bed or battlefield. Still, I realized that I must rise to the challenge.

"Shall I call him out, to prove who's the better man?" I asked.

"Don Felipe is forbidden to duel on English soil," she said. "He's considered much too valuable in Madrid."

Again I had the shrewd suspicion that she was teasing me. "What you've told me today is desolating enough," I said. "Don't make matters worse by inventing another suitor: you know we were meant for each other."

"So we were, *querido*. There are times when I feel I can't live without you."

The words seemed to come from the depths of her being. It shocked me beyond measure to realize she meant them—that all she had said before (including her coquettish hint that De Vera might become her lover) had been mere lagniappe, to cozen me into a declaration from which there would be no retreating.

"How often must I say I'll sue for your hand the moment I'm worthy?"

The answer seemed to satisfy her. "Remember I've given my pledge to Raleigh," I continued, pressing my advantage. "Think what you like of him, he's made fortunes in his time. Only yesterday he swore there is gold in Virginia, and promised me my share——"

"El Dorado is on Trinidad's doorstep," she said. "And my uncle is governor of Trinidad."

"Does Don Antonio de Berreo know the path to El Dorado?"

"He has talked to the caciques from the land beyond the Orenoque," said Elvira, her eyes bright with excitement. "I've even heard that he will soon have possession of a map."

This was hardly news to me; trails to the City of Gold had been traced for the past century—ever since the voyages of Columbus had proved the existence of the precious metal in the New World. Pablo had told me he was prepared to guide Raleigh to the spot himself. . . . I saw instantly that Elvira's statement was only bait to lure me further: yet I could hardly fail to respond in kind.

"Would your uncle trust his map to a visitor from Ireland?"

"I'm not without influence in that quarter, Shawn. What if I persuaded him to let you lead an expedition into the Orenoque valley? If you found gold there you could ask for my hand as your reward. Tío Antonio would give me the richest dowry in Christendom——"

"You're a temptress beyond the dreams of avarice," I told her solemnly. "But I've given my pledge to Raleigh. Would you have me dishonor it?"

"No, Shawn—not if it means that much to you." She rose with the words and stepped out of the gazebo, then turned to me with a pleading smile. "I didn't mean to love you," she whispered. "I thought I'd sport with you for a while and be none the worse for it. Now, God help me, the barb has struck."

God help us both, I thought. Aloud, I said only, "At least we've a little time before you leave England."

"We'll make the most of it, Shawn. I promise you that."

I watched her cross the greensward of Whitehall, with her proud, dark head held high. Never would I have thought myself capable of pitying Elvira Quesada—but I found that I could sorrow for her today. The barb of Amor had struck her, and she would never be the same. With the same barb in my own flesh, but from another source, I could picture her suffering perfectly.

CHAPTER X

The Comedy of Errors

THE NIGHT of our production of Will Shakespeare's new play (at the Queen's old palace in Greenwich), though it was over a fortnight after my adventure at Whitehall, arrived with indecent speed. All through Christmas week we were in a fever of preparation—rehearsing our lines and business until we were letter-perfect, then moving our scenery down-river to the palace landing. Such precautions were necessary for a command performance. The Queen was an ardent lover of the drama and a merciless critic. We could afford no flubbed speeches, or the danger of boring her—affronts which monarchs the world over are unlikely to forgive or forget.

I had received no further summons to court. Cecil advised me to be patient. Elizabeth would send for me again, he vowed, when the mood was on her. Somehow I could face that prospect without fear. My contact with Her Majesty, brief though it had been, had convinced me that she was as human as myself—and as eager for new horizons.

Raleigh's flotilla was at anchor in Plymouth harbor, awaiting its sailing orders. Colonists had been recruited all over England and stood ready to go aboard: that, too, was part of Raleigh's refusal to take the dark view. Once he had launched a project, it was already completed in his mind. Save for his setback at court, he had suffered but few failures—the loss of the Virginia colony being by far the most severe. For this reason he was doubly eager to press his new assault.

I was brooding on these matters when Susanna and I boarded the barge that would float us down-river to Greenwich Palace. All during the afternoon I had helped to load the portmanteaus filled with costumes. Now, as the boatmen cast off their lines, I took a seat beside her in the bow. It was our first real moment alone since the night in the sewing room.

True, we shared the barge with several apprentice actors, who were chattering at the rail and pointing out the dwellings of the great as we passed. But we were seated apart from them —and the fact that Susanna had not stirred at my approach seemed a favorable sign. So did the guileless look she gave me as I began to speak of indifferent things; the property list she was checking at the moment, the icy perfection of the winter afternoon.

"Don't talk," she said, "if the words stick in your craw."

"What would you have from me, Puss? Ask me what you like."

"Are you happy here?"

"I've learned my place," I said carefully. "They say it's all one can expect of the young."

Her eyes widened. "And what under heaven does *that* signify?"

"Put it this way. Two months ago I came to London, with a

head full of poetry I'll never write. God help me, I thought I had only to belabor my muse a bit to surpass Master Will. I see now that I'll never be a dramatist—much less an actor."

Puss tossed her head and studied the wheeling gulls above the Thames. "Why stay on, then?"

"Because I belong to the Theatre—and hope to have my own playhouse someday. Or a share in the Globe, at least. Don't call it a dream. It *could* come true."

"So it could, Master Shawn—if you find El Dorado."

At the Theatre I'd made no secret of the fact I was pledged to sail with Raleigh. Her coldness shocked me nonetheless.

"All men seek El Dorado," I said.

"You know it's a myth."

"The New World is a place where myths come true. Suppose we *do* find the Golden Ones and their golden city. D'you fault me for going, Puss?"

"No, Master Irishman. When I first clapped eyes on you I saw you had an itching foot."

"Don't think I'll be gone forever. I'll repay all the Theatre has given me."

"Make us no promises you can't keep. You won't be wearing the buskin on your return. Not if you marry Mistress Quesada. She'd never permit it."

"Who said I intended to marry her?"

"Never mind who said it."

It was on the tip of my tongue to confess everything—including the game I'd been playing in Elvira's arms. But I restrained the impulse; it was unlikely that Susanna would believe me in her present mood. "There are things I can't discuss," I said firmly. "My relations with Doña Elvira is one."

"It's no secret you're bedmates."

"That, too, is a matter I can't explain."

"Doesn't it explain itself?"

"There's more to our relations than meets the eye."

"I'm sure of that," she flared. "Even in London there's a little decency left."

"Think what you like of me. But I'll never marry her. Someday I'll tell you why."

"Tell me now, Shawn MacManus."

"I can't—not while I'm in Raleigh's service." Seeing that I was emerging a poor second best in this duel of tongues, I left her—as quickly as I could—to help shift our boxes to the Greenwich quay.

Fortunately for us both, we were plunged at once into the myriad tasks that attend the mounting of a new play, and thus had no chance to wound each other further. When the heralds lifted their trumpets at last, we were too tired for insults and stood together in the wings in what could only be called a silent truce. From this spot, thanks to the nature of our present stage, it was possible to eavesdrop on the audience, which was a small one because of the restricted size of the hall.

The Queen sat on her usual dais in a brocaded armchair, with her lords and ladies about her. I picked out Cecil at once, standing just behind the royal presence. Essex, as befitted his position, was at Elizabeth's right hand, whispering busily whenever he could catch her attention. As the play proceeded, however, I was glad to note that she had rapped him sharply (with the great plumed fan she was carrying), a sure sign that her attention was riveted to the stage.

This was the first time I had seen a play presented after dark. Jaimie and I had arranged masses of candles in a semicircle before the acting space, so that it was bathed in light. It was easy to deduce, from the rapt, sighing response of the audience, that the feeling of reality (which is the goal of every dramatist) is easier to achieve in such circumstances. While the magic lasted, it was almost as if the stage were a universe with a heartbeat of its own—upon which the audience looked from a great distance, though we could almost touch across that half-moon of radiance.

Shakespeare felt the response to his finger ends. When he stalked into the wings for his last scene he was all but dancing with delight.

"Hear that silence, lad?" he whispered. "It proves they love us as they never loved themselves. D'you guess why?"

"I think so, Master Will."

"Tonight we've shown 'em a finer world than *they'll* ever know—for all their pomp and circumstance. We've lifted 'em out of themselves and purged their souls of evil. 'Tis what Aristotle called the divine catharsis."

"Divine is the word, sir," I agreed heartily. "Tell me, why does a play act better by candlelight?"

"For two reasons. The theater is a thing of artifice—an illusion more real than life. 'Tis always easier to deceive by candlelight, whether you're woman or dramatist."

"And the second reason?"

"Listen, and you'll have the answer. A play is a love affair between actors and listeners. The passion we share tonight is a flower that grows best in the dark."

"Perhaps we'll soon be building playhouses indoors then," I said.

"Without the open pit? Where would you put our groundlings?"

"Why not build a sloping floor—with rows of benches, so every spectator could see the stage clearly? Those nearest the actors could pay the most. What we now call groundlings could use the galleries."

"An audacious idea, lad. We won't see it in our lifetime."

"Why not build such a theater when we plan the Globe?"

He gave me a startled look. "Have you voted yourself a partner to that enterprise?"

"If you'll have me, sir."

"Bring back enough gold from New Spain, and we'll give your fancy free play," said the dramatist, and stalked on stage as he heard his cue.

The performance ended in a thunder of applause and much bowing behind the candles. Afterward Her Majesty sent word that the members of the company were to be presented to her, a sure sign that she was pleased by our work. Shepherded by chamberlains, we filed into the hall in a solemn row, with Shakespeare and Burbage in the van. I held back purposely until the last, with only Susanna preceding me. When the girl stepped forward to make her curtsy I was pleased by her aplomb. Remembering my own fidgets at Whitehall, I could applaud her coolness, for I knew she was trembling inwardly.

Elizabeth leaned forward when she saw Puss. I could have sworn that she had noted my presence behind her.

"So here's a true girl at last, milords," she said. "And a pretty piece to boot. How are ye called, lass?"

"Susanna, Your Majesty," said Puss, with her eyes demurely low. "Susanna Field."

"A Puritan, are you not?"

"I was born as one, ma'am," said the girl—and I could feel the terror in her voice. The Queen's hatred for that bluenose sect was a legend in London, since she was continually at loggerheads with its members in the city council. I knew how the old woman's rage could blaze up at the most trival cause—in this case the fact that a Puritan (or rather the descendant of one) had ventured into her presence. It was clear that only a strong counter-irritant could save Puss from the royal displeasure, and I stepped forward to offer it.

"May I inform Your Majesty that Susanna designed all our costumes tonight—and sewed most of them?"

The diversion worked, for the Queen swiveled in her chair. "And who, sirrah, are you?"

I offered her a belated bow. "Shawn MacManus, Your Majesty," I said. "At Whitehall you asked that I be presented to you again."

The hall was deathly still after I had spoken. I glanced toward Essex's chair and was relieved to observe that he had departed. Cecil (who now stood behind the Queen) was pulling at his long upper lip as though he could not quite choose between a chuckle or a frown. As for Elizabeth herself, her expression was startling. First, she turned red as any turkey cock—and I could feel the walls of the Tower close round me. Then I caught the light of recognition in her eyes, even before she burst into another roar of mirth.

"The Irishman," she shouted. "The impudent Irishman, who looks so much like Wat Raleigh!"

I bowed over the hand she extended. (Under cover of the obeisance, I shot a quick wink at Susanna, who made a second, even deeper curtsy.) "The pleasure is all the greater, ma'am," I said, "because it was unforeseen."

"Plague take your smooth tongue, boy," she said, and, for the first time, she did not bellow but addressed me in the relaxed tone one uses to an equal. "Don't think you'll turn my wrath from this doxy."

"Susanna did not mean to offend, Your Majesty."

"She offended nonetheless. Puritans are not welcome at Greenwich Palace."

"Or in England, ma'am," said Puss. "My father knows that well. That's why he plans to take me to the New World."

It was my turn to gasp at what I could only call an audacious invention. But the Queen seemed far from displeased.

"So you'd seek your fortune overseas," she said. "Can't you find a husband nearer home?"

"The New World is the England of tomorrow, ma'am,"

said Susanna. "Perhaps the Puritans can worship God as they please there. As for husbands"—she lifted her eyes, and gave the Queen a most roguish smile—"I'm told they're always plentiful in a virgin land."

"Have it your way, Mistress Field," said Elizabeth. "How d'you propose to make the journey?"

"With Sir Walter Raleigh's flotilla," said Puss calmly. "If it's true that he's sailing."

"Raleigh's been given no patent—and I've no mind to grant one."

"At the Theatre, Your Majesty, they're saying he'd be gone only long enough to establish a colony. All of us are praying you'll let him sail."

"Give me a reason, girl——"

"You'd christen the England of tomorrow," said Susanna. "Isn't that reason enough?"

"Raleigh's already named a wilderness after me," said Elizabeth. "It proved a graveyard for all who ventured there."

"We might prosper this time—with God's help."

"I've no ships to spare."

"Sir Walter will found the colony at his own expense."

"You seem privy to his plans, my girl. Who keeps you informed?"

"Master MacManus, Your Majesty. 'Tis he who persuaded my father and me to cast our lot with Sir Walter."

The Queen swiveled her head in my direction, with the abrupt, birdlike motion that was part of her. "So you're the devil's advocate, Master Shawn. I might have guessed it."

I could only incline my head in silent assent. Susanna's improvisation had left me too breathless to speak.

"You feel that Englishmen should risk their lives beyond the seas?"

"They've done so since the time of Sir Francis Drake, Your Majesty."

"You'd sail with Raleigh if I permitted it?"

"I'm pledged to the venture, ma'am. I don't break promises."

Elizabeth got to her feet. "So you keep your promises," she said slowly. Her mind seemed far away as she spoke. Though she addressed me directly, she might have forgotten my presence. "That makes you a jewel among men—a jewel indeed."

"Forgive me if I spoke my mind, ma'am," I said.

"I forgive you freely, Shawn MacManus," said the Queen. "In fact, ye have my blessing—the pair of you."

She glanced at Susanna and seemed about to speak further. Instead she took the arm that Cecil offered and left the hall, walking with the slow, regal solemnity for which she was famous. There were more bows and curtsies as she passed— then a silence broken by a snarl of trumpets, a signal that the royal audience had ended.

Susanna flounced into the wings as the doors sighed shut on the Queen's departure. I gave chase instantly, my crotchets forgotten for once. The stage was in dusty hubbub as our apprentices sweated at the task of striking our scenery. In the confusion she led me a pretty chase before I prisoned her at last at the gangplank of our barge. Even there, she all but escaped me until I trapped her with a grip on one wrist.

"Let me go, Shawn!"

"Why'd you behave as you did?"

"I was trying to help you."

"Can't you see you may have ruined everything?"

"How? You were presented at Whitehall to plead Raleigh's cause."

"You might have let me plead it in my fashion."

"Isn't that what you did—before the whole court?"

"You saw how she left——"

"After giving us her blessing."

"What use is a Queen's blessing?"

"I'll wager a shilling to a penny that Sir Walter gets his patent. If he does, he'll have me to thank."

"She's heard the arguments a dozen times," I said. "Every friend Sir Walter has at court, from Cecil down, has urged her to send him on another voyage, and she's turned a deaf ear. Why should she hearken to *us*?"

"Not to us, Shawn—to you."

"But why?"

"You remind the lady of her youth, Master Irishman. In your presence she feels young again. Believe me, it's a precious gift for any woman. See you bestow it wisely."

She had wrenched herself free before I could detain her. In sober truth I had no desire to continue the argument. I had already sensed the presence of a man-at-arms at my elbow and knew in advance what message he brought.

"Her Majesty is in her closet, sir. She desires your presence for a game of chess."

The fellow went clanking down the quay almost before the message was out, assuming, as a matter of course, that I would follow. I cast a final glance toward the barge, which had already begun to move into the Thames with a great churning of oar blades. I could not quite pick out Susanna's face in the darkness—but there was no mistaking her voice.

"Try the Queen's gambit, Shawn. It's one way of winning."

CHAPTER XI

Queen's Gambit

CHESS IS a game at which I have excelled since child-hood. At the Theatre I had played often with Bur-bage and other members of the company, and met none who could best me. Tonight, while I followed the Queen's man-at-arms, I will admit that I had never approached a board with less stomach for the contest—if, indeed, Elizabeth had sum-moned me to match wits at chess.

Distraught as I was, I scarcely noted the splendors of the rooms through which we passed; the corridor where suits of armor stood in rows (like the ghosts of long-dead crusaders), a banquet hall where the night wind moaned at a half-open casement. Beyond this hall was a second gallery, then, a square stone antechamber. A half dozen guards leaped to at-tention at our footsteps, then slumped on their benches again when they recognized my guide.

The hall was spacious, with a high-vaulted ceiling. A half story above the flagstones a flight of stairs ended on a balcony, where other uniformed shadows stood guard. My guide paused at the bottom step and bowed me on my way. The men at the door flung the portal open and stood aside. Advancing cautiously, I found myself in a second, far smaller antechamber, bare of decoration save a tapestry or two, and lit by a pair of roaring fires. The Queen's own closet was just beyond, accessible through an archway. A transparent curtain hung here, giving the visitor the illusion that he was viewing the snug, richly furnished apartment through a water glass.

I paused on this second threshold, uncertain if I should announce myself by knocking. Somehow I had not expected to gain the royal presence so easily. It boded ill for the evening if our game was to be played without even a tiring maid as onlooker. The half-open door in the far wall of the closet could open only to a boudoir. (I could make out the silhouette of a bed whose overstuffed mattress might have slept a whole corporal's guard.) I remembered Susanna's final challenge from the barge and stiffened my backbone.

Come what may, I told myself, you can't fail Raleigh now.

"Is it you, Irishman?"

The Queen's voice, booming through the half-open door, rocked me on my heels. Had we been friends of long standing, she could not have offered a more cavalier greeting—or one less calculated to put me at ease.

"Here, Your Majesty."

"Then come in, boy, and study out your game. I'll join you in a moment."

I pushed the curtains aside and entered the closet. It was a small room and an intimate one, with a carpet of piled doeskins and family paintings on every wall. In one corner stood a facsimile of the world, which the voyages of Magellan and Drake had long since proved to be round, though there are ignorant folk who still think otherwise. I had heard of this huge globe, which had been fashioned as a special novelty for the Queen. It dominated the room, like the soothsayer's crystal it resembled.

I moved to the globe and twirled it until the confused land mass called America came into view. Here, thrust like a malformed nose into the archipelago of the Western Indies, was the territory that Spain called Florida. So vague was the chart that I could not estimate where it ended and Virginia began. It was easy to see why the dons (who are always dogs-in-the-manger) should claim the whole of it, because of the bastion they called St. Augustine, and the missionary journeys of their friars to the north and west of that puny fortress town.

I was still pondering the facts of geography when I heard the rustle of silk behind me. Elizabeth had entered the room so quietly that I had not noticed. She was wearing a white cymar, a billowing *robe de nuit* with edgings of fur at sleeves and neck. Her bright red hair was unbound, and hung nearly to her waist. For an instant I felt sure that I was facing another woman. The jeweled and painted virago of the throne-chair had vanished without a trace; in her stead was a smiling, warm-eyed creature whose head scarce reached my shoulder— and who seemed, to my startled mind, as frail (and as defenseless) as any virgin.

Just in time I remembered my court bow. I also recalled Will Shakespeare's warning that candlelight is a woman's best ally.

"Well, Master Shawn!" she cried. "I suggested you plan your game—and now I find you mooning over New Spain. Are you so confident of besting me?"

The booming voice did much to restore my poise. In flowing silk, with her tresses unbound and the light behind her, Elizabeth Tudor had brought back (at least for an instant) the image of her girlhood. Nothing could disguise the old Queen's voice—the imperious bark that for more than thirty years had proclaimed her mastery.

"It is Virginia I study, Your Majesty, not New Spain," I told her boldly. "Or should I say the future, not the past?"

She joined me at the globe, and I had my first whiff of the musky perfume she was wearing. There were cynics in London who said that their Queen never bathed, that she used lotions to disguise the stink of her body—but this (as I know from firsthand observation) was a lie. Tonight she had obviously come straight from tub to chessboard, pausing just long enough to toss the cymar about her. The perfume was a cachet, not a lure to rouse my senses.

Or so I hoped, while she let her eyes stray over the map— bending a bit closer to spell out its contours until the whole New World was enclosed in the flaming tent of her hair.

"So you'd go to Virginia, Master Shawn," she said. "Do you plan to hold it for England?"

"For my Queen," I said. "I'm still an Irishman."

"You'll take the lass—as your wife?"

My memory fumbled at the declarations Susanna had made after the play. I sensed that I was walking a high wire, with no net to catch me if I stumbled. After all, Puss had said that both she and her father were enrolled among Raleigh's colonists. This was no time to deny the story.

"Such is my intention, ma'am," I lied—as steadily as I could.

"You believe, then, that England's future lies beyond the Ocean Sea?"

"If we use our wits, and the courage that's in us, we can girdle this globe with colonies someday." I dared to give the huge, unwieldy sphere a twirl, to underline the boldness of my vision.

"Only if we're strong at home, lad."

"Stronger than King Philip, ma'am?"

"I've spent a lifetime healing England's wounds, settling England's faith—and uniting England round its throne. There's been no time for such junkets as Raleigh is forever planning. I need him as a defender of the realm, not as a colonist."

"Your Majesty, England will always be a small, embattled nation if you won't extend her domain."

"D'you contradict me to my face, Shawn MacManus?"

"I'm not a courtier, ma'am. When I say you're the greatest sovereign this land has known, I speak from the heart. But England still hesitates on the doorsill of a new age. Only you can make her take the next step forward. Would you hold back, for fear of King Philip?"

"I fear no man—that dusty spider least of all. So far I've played his game and won every trick. I've scuttled his Armada; I've plundered him at will, when my treasury needed gold. What's more, I'll live to see his empire crumble."

"So you will," I said, "if you'll let Raleigh challenge him in the New World."

She raised a jeweled fist as though she would strike me across the mouth. Instead, the fingers uncurled slowly until they had cupped my chin and brought her face level with mine. For a small eternity we stood thus while she studied me with those imperious eyes. Then she moved even closer, until her lips (it was odd how young they seemed, now she had washed away the paint) just missed brushing my own.

For a moment, I was positive she meant to buss me—and wondered if it was a reward for my plain speaking. Then, with a bark of laughter, she dropped her hold and moved to the table that stood before the fire.

"Enough of empire building, Master Shawn," she said. "I'll

hear no more stories of Utopia. Not until I've proved I'm the best chess player in England."

As we took our places on opposite sides of the board, I saw that she had chosen the whites, which gave her the first move. I had heard many stories of the games she played here. It was said that she and Essex battled at cards almost nightly (from what I knew of the crafty earl, I could guess that he contrived to lose in the closet that he might win in the boudoir). For my part, I felt that I had won the first round when I dared to contest her judgment.

The set of chessmen was a thing of beauty, carved ivory pieces that must have come from Cathay. I matched the Queen's first move (a pawn to king's fourth) and settled back to study the game of which she was so proud. Two moves later I saw that she was using the rudimentary scholar's mate as her attack, and realized that her chess had more flash than depth. After we had traded bishops for knights, and I had avoided a dozen traps she set for me, any true expert would have wagered I could outwit her. . . .

Cecil had told me that the Queen faced him often across the board and had yet to lose a match. Raleigh himself (who had contested here often when he was a familiar of her closet) had vowed that Elizabeth's chess had no peer. Judging by my own experience, I could only conclude that neither gentleman had taken time to master the game.

I permitted our first contest to end in a draw, after a long battle that swept aside nearly all the pieces, leaving only kings, queens, and a single rook apiece. As I had expected, the Queen fell into an ominous silence when she saw victory elude her—save for an occasional oath that might have startled the men-at-arms outside her door. These were the obvious marks of the bad loser, a failing from which few sovereigns are spared.

While we set up the second board I wondered if I dared continue with my plan. Yet, if I did not fight her all the way, how could I convince her that I was a friend she could trust?

"Come, lad," she snarled. "Leave off your gawking and open your game."

I remembered Susanna's advice and attacked with the queen's gambit. This is an approach that involves the queen and both knights; it can end a game in some eight moves if one's opponent is innocent enough. Its key is the deliberate sacrifice of the attacker's queen, which opens the way for checkmate.

When it was my turn to make the vital sacrifice Elizabeth had done little to advance her own attack, beyond a routine development of her pawns. I fiddled intentionally with the piece before placing it in jeopardy—then, with the move half made, I kept my hand on the ivory figure, giving her every chance to warn me that I risked its loss, a customary courtesy of the game. Elizabeth said nothing, so I completed the move and sat back. I caught the feral gleam in her eye when she noted what seemed a blunder. The familiar, near-male laughter rumbled in her throat even before her hand darted forward to capture my most powerful piece.

"For shame, lad!" she crowed. "Is that how you use queens in Ireland?"

"I'm afraid so, ma'am—when victory's at stake." As I spoke I hopped my knight into her second line of defense, to capture a pawn for checkmate.

She went red in a flash, and I feared her eyes would leap from their sockets. Then she composed herself with a mighty effort and smote the board with her fist.

" 'Twas a low trick, Master Shawn," she shouted. "It succeeded only because my mind was elsewhere."

"Chess is no game for divided thoughts, ma'am. Will you take the whites?"

"I will indeed, Irishman. And I won't be diddled again."

She almost proved her boast with the third game, which she played with a dogged concentration that approached brilliance. In the end, a rash threat by her queen permitted me to capture a rook and end matters with a checkmate that left her almost speechless with rage. This time she swept the board aside, so violently that it split down the middle.

I dropped to hands and knees to retrieve her chessmen before the fire could damage them. In an instant she was on the floor beside me, helping to restore the pieces to their box. I realized that she was laughing, despite the blue blaze of curses that whistled through her teeth.

"Did my temper feaze ye, lad?"

"No, Your Majesty," I said calmly—for I was beginning to understand her at last. "After all, the provocation was great."

"How so?"

"You're an excellent player. 'Tis hardly your fault you met a master."

Elizabeth Tudor settled before the fire and hugged her knees. In that pose she looked small and oddly vulnerable. Just in time I restrained the impulse to put an arm around her—to comfort her because she was a woman alone, in a world of men who could never say her nay.

"For two straws I'd keep you by me a while," she said. "If only to remind myself that my sense of humor hasn't quite left me. But I'm sending you back. After all, your first duty's to Raleigh, not to me."

"I've tried to plead his cause," I said. "Forgive me if I passed the bounds of decorum."

"Tell me this before you go, Shawn. Did you rebel when he sent you to persuade me?"

"Only at first," I said. "And then, only because I was afraid."

"I thought the Irish feared nothing."

"All of us fear we'll be unworthy of a trust," I said. "It seems I've bungled mine."

"What makes you feel that?"

"Surely I've failed as Sir Walter's advocate. This expedition to the New World is the one thing nearest his heart—yet you refuse him permission to sail."

"Who says I refused? True, I made you argue your cause—and seemed to close my mind to the arguments. Can't you see that I was testing you?"

"Was the chess game part of the test?"

"Of course. Don't think I wouldn't have noticed if you were yielding an inch to me." She scowled before she turned to me again and laid a hand on my arm. "Not that I'll admit you're the better player. It's only that luck was with you tonight."

"Forgive me if I'm still rude," I said, "but when did Your Majesty decide to grant us the patent?"

"Tonight, at the play's end," she said. "When you championed that pert young miss whose tongue's as sharp as yours."

"Then Susanna convinced you—as much as I?"

"Put it this way, lad. You speak of England's future, as against England's past. You're part of that future. So is the girl. My task is to make sure you'll be leading better lives when I'm in my grave. Perhaps the grass is really greener across the Ocean Sea. I don't doubt the horizons are wider. If Raleigh can make homes for you there, I give you leave to sail."

I remembered what Susanna had said when we parted on the quay. Puss, it seemed, had understood our sovereign far better than I. It piqued me somewhat to admit that she had tipped the scales in Raleigh's favor—and I forced myself to utter as much of the truth as I dared.

"We may not be her permanent colonists, ma'am," I said. "I hope for a career in the London theater. So does Susanna."

"Have it, then—after you've taken your share of gold. In the New World it grows under every bush."

"We'll try to justify that faith, Your Majesty."

"So you will, Shawn MacManus. Even if you fail, I'll not hold it against you."

"And Sir Walter?"

Her face darkened. For a moment, at least, she was the bitter crone with whom I'd crossed swords at Whitehall.

"You've done your best for Raleigh," she said. "He's schemed a long time to conquer America. If *he* returns empty-handed, we'll have his head."

I got to my feet, taking her shift to the regal "we" as a sign I should go. When she held out both hands to me, I lifted her until we stood eye to eye.

"What are ye thinking now, lad?"

"Only this, ma'am. When they made you the mold was broken."

"I'll take that for my epitaph, Irishman," she said. "Now get about your business, before you cozen me completely."

Cecil awaited me in the antechamber, with a courier's pouch beneath his arm. He led me by another route to the palace courtyard. We did not speak until the coach that would return me to London rumbled into view. Even then, as I took my seat within, he was careful to thrust his head through the window, lest the postilions overhear.

" 'Twas a good night's work, Shawn MacManus."

"She promised Raleigh his patent, sir. When will she send it?"

"It went out an hour ago, by special courier. It should reach Plymouth tomorrow."

So the Queen had made her mind up, even before she summoned me. Susanna, not I, had decided her.

"Her Majesty has been most generous," I murmured.

"When she moves she moves fast," said Cecil, with a twinkle in those fine scholar's eyes.

"Should I follow the courier to Plymouth?"

"You've time to give your notice at the Theatre, and to say your farewells. Raleigh is dividing the flotilla at the Canaries. His own flagship won't weigh anchor until he's finished victualing." Cecil laid the leather pouch on my knee. "Besides, you've a courier's task of your own to perform in London. Don't tell me that you've forgotten Don Pedro de Quesada?"

"No, milord. Is this our final message for the King of Spain?"

"It's a forgery of the patent. Read it on the way." Cecil's long horse-face was not built for smiling, but it now wore something very like a grin. "By the way—who won at chess?"

"Forgive me, sir," I said, "but that's a question I refuse to answer."

My heart was dancing its own rigadoon when the coach rolled from the palace yard; I was bubbling over with the same wild release when we stopped under the archway of Quesada's manse. I knew he would welcome my intrusion, despite the late hour. Nor was I surprised to note that the windows of a ground-floor room (which Elvira had once identified as the scoundrel's study) glowed with light. Your Spaniard works best in the dark, behind drawn blinds.

I had made friends with Quesada's coachman; it seemed a good augury that he should open the door tonight in answer to my knock, rather than the ferret-nosed butler.

"Is your master in, Enrique?"

"Does he expect you, señor?" If the fellow was surprised to find me at the *sala* door (instead of the postern) he gave no sign.

"He'll welcome me when he hears my news." I pressed a gold piece into the coachman's palm. "Tell him I bring tidings from Greenwich Palace."

My estimate was accurate. In another moment Quesada was bustling into his entrance hall to welcome me, looking like a molting owl in an untidy dressing sack.

"Bring us wine, Enrique, and see we aren't disturbed," he ordered, and led the way into his study. To my surprise, I saw that the room was stripped almost bare, save for the candle sconces and a table stacked high with papers. Quesada waved me to a seat on a packing box.

"Are you leaving London, sir?"

"I'm afraid I must, Master Shawn," he said in English. "My position here grows daily more untenable."

"And your niece?"

"Elvira sailed yesterday for Cádiz. She'll take ship there for the New World."

I felt a stir of uneasiness far back in my brain—the spot that is the first to come alive when I am faced with a fact I cannot explain. Elvira's departure was no real shock, in the light of our long talk at Whitehall. What disturbed me was the manner of her leaving. And then, even as I brought the question into the open, the answer suggested itself. My siren still desired me as a husband—enough to quit England in this mysterious fashion, hoping it would stir my jealousy.

"I trust your niece is well attended," I said. "These are dangerous times for travelers."

"Her escort is Don Felipe de Vera. He goes to Trinidad to serve as her uncle's military aide."

The picture was clear now: I needed but one question more. "Will Doña Elvira reside there also?"

"At the seat of government, called Port-of-Spain." The eyes under those snow-white brows regarded me sharply. "Why do you ask? Is Raleigh bound for Trinidad as well?"

"No, señor. I've news of Sir Walter's plans in this pouch. They do not include Trinidad."

I had scanned the forged patent in the coach. Now, as I put it in Quesada's hands, I could afford to study him at my leisure while he read it through. The forgery gave Raleigh leave to sail for Virginia, by any route he chose. It forbade him, in specific terms, to touch at any other land en route, save to provision his ships. Furthermore, he was told to proceed to the site he had chosen with diligence, and to devote his entire energies to establishing his colony. . . . Had King Philip himself selected our settlement in the New World, he could not have isolated it more completely from his own domains.

Quesada, I noted, was racing through the forgery again, as though he meant to burn each word into his memory. "This could not have reached me at a better time, Master Shawn," he said. "I feared I must go back to Madrid a defeated man. May I make a copy?"

"Of course, sir."

Watching his quill race across the foolscap, I wondered what he would have given for a look at Elizabeth's actual patent. This document gave Raleigh a virtual *carte blanche*. He was enjoined by his sovereign to "offend and enfeeble the King of Spain, and to discover and subdue heathen lands not in the possession of any Christian prince, or inhabited by any Christian people." Further, he was empowered to "resist and to expel any person who should attempt to settle within two hundred leagues of the place he fixed upon as a settlement."

With such general orders, the expedition could drop anchor in any roadstead its commander chose. The Queen had made no specific recommendation in the patent. However, Cecil had told me that a private letter (which accompanied the original document) ordered Raleigh to touch at Guiana, and to plant a colony there if the situation warranted it. Elizabeth also desired that he explore the Orenoque River and its tributaries, to affirm, or to deny, the existence of Manoa, and the Golden Ones.

Thus our purpose was threefold. Our first task was to establish a settlement in the very shadow of the Spanish dominion of Trinidad. Our second was to secure it by force of arms, which almost surely meant a surprise attack on Port-of-Spain. Finally we must open the treasures of Guiana to England, even if it meant the conquest of the Golden Ones and their fabled empire.

It was a perilous venture, even a fantastic one—but the rewards could be incalculable. Its timing, of course, was vital; Madrid must remain ignorant of our true motives until the last possible moment. This had been my special assignment—and, from the look on Quesada's face as he copied the last word of the forgery, I dared to hope I had succeeded.

The Spaniard rose from his writing table at last, sanded the foolscap, and returned the courier's pouch to me. Then, without a word, he opened a strongbox and tossed me a fat purse. Understanding him as I did, I took this as my accolade.

"Thanks again, Master Shawn," he said in his high, lisping Castilian. "Your aid has been invaluable."

I balanced the purse in both my hands: it was too heavy to

hold in one. "I'm glad the laborer was worthy of his hire, señor."

"I regret you can't deliver these facts to His Most Catholic Majesty in person. He'd give you higher rewards than gold."

"I, too, would like to visit Spain," I told him, exploiting my advantage further. "There's no point in hiding the regard I feel for Doña Elvira——"

"Join me, then. I hardly think your suit would go unrewarded."

"I can't leave Raleigh now," I said, with a show of reluctance. "He'd draw his own conclusion if he learned I was quitting London with you."

"You're right, of course. He must never know how well you've served me."

"I'll not detain you further then, Don Pedro. I can see you've much to do before morning."

"So I have, *amigo mío*. Go with God."

"*Vaya con Dios, señor.*"

I left him with that pious farewell an unwelcome echo in my ears—yet it was somehow fitting that we should part as we had met, on a lie. It had strained my conscience to profess a love for Elvira, but that, too, was essential to the double game I'd played so shrewdly.

Dawn was breaking on the Strand. Once again I rattled through London in a fine coach, on my way to the pallet I had called home, in the Theatre's sewing room. This time I prayed that Susanna would admit me. With Quesada leaving London, and Raleigh's sails already spread, I could tell her everything—including the reasons behind my affair with Elvira. Once that sorry confession was behind me, I could ask her to await my return from Guiana.

A dramatist even now (though I'd forsaken the muse for more mundane pursuits), I found myself composing tag ends of dialogue to implement my suit. Perhaps—if I was eloquent enough—she would listen for once without laughing. I would ask no more of her than a promise to wait and a good-by kiss that I would take as both pardon and absolution.

But there was no sign of Puss when I reached the Theatre. I was told that she and her father had long since retired to the quarters they shared above the stage door. I could not quite bring myself to rout her out. Tired though I was, I made myself pitch in and help store the scenery we had brought back from Greenwich. Then, when the last apprentice had straggled out for breakfast, I sought my couch at last.

Perhaps I was more exhausted than I knew, for the day was far advanced when I wakened. No play was listed for that afternoon, and the unaccustomed silence had lulled me. The only sound that reached the sewing room as I rubbed the sleep from my eyelids was the thud of a buskin on the stage beyond.

I shook myself into wakefulness. A glance at the scrap of mirror on the door told me that I was presentable—enough so, at any rate, to face Susanna Field and declare my love. Yet I did not go to the stage alley at once. Instead, I entered the Theatre by the wings, where I could watch the one-man rehearsing of Master Richard Burbage.

Today he was working in full costume (it was his method, as the role he was creating took its final form). I needed but a few lines to realize that he was declaiming the part of Romeo, from the lovers' tragedy that Master Will would soon unveil for the first time. It was the moment when Romeo, having risked his life to enter the Capulets' garden, spies Juliet dreaming at her casement. We actors had long since dubbed it the balcony scene.

> *Arise, fair sun, and kill the envious moon,*
> *Who is already sick and pale with grief,*
> *That thou, her maid, art far more fair than she:*
> *Be not her maid, since she is envious;*
> *Her vestal livery is but sick and green*
> *And none but fools do wear it; Cast it off!*

The last line, delivered in a whisper, was accompanied by a windmill gesture; it sent Burbage half across the stage, until he was face to face with me. Charmed as I was by his reading, I had had no wish to interrupt. Now my presence shocked the actor back into the everyday.

"So you're up at last, Shawn," he said. His natural voice seemed oddly colorless after the poetry he had just declaimed so movingly. "I looked in at noon and hadn't the heart to waken you."

"May I be of service, sir?"

"No, lad. I realize your stint here has ended, now that

fairer fields are beckoning. It's only that I had a message from Puss——"

It was unlike Susanna to address me through another. "Where is she, Master Dick—that she can't speak for herself?"

"At this moment I'd say she and Jamie were halfway to Plymouth."

"*Plymouth*, sir?"

"They rode out at midnight," said Burbage. "Puss asked me to say good-by for them both. They wished to be in good time to join Raleigh."

"D'you mean they're sailing with the colonists?"

"Jaimie signed the articles the day after you fought with Fitzraugh. They asked me to keep it a secret."

CHAPTER XII

Across the Ocean Sea

RIDING INTO the night with Pablo, rising in the dawn to drive our mounts across western England, we galloped into Plymouth in an angry red sunset that held a threat of snow. A storm gnawed the sea beyond the harbor, where a few of Raleigh's ships still rode at anchor. As I had feared, the vessels bearing the colonists had long since departed, and were now en route for the Canaries. It was their plan to rendezvous offshore with the other (and faster) ships. Knowing the Queen's penchant for changing her mind, Raleigh had taken no chances. By sending the colonists ahead, he had committed the whole venture before Elizabeth could thwart him, as she had on other occasions.

During my headlong ride I had moved too fast for conscious planning. My chief purpose (since I knew the hazards we were facing) had been to dissuade Susanna from making the voyage—or, if persuasion failed, to ask Raleigh to deny her passage. As I say, my hopes for success had been small. From what Dick Burbage had told me, it was evident that Puss had laid her plans carefully; in short, that she had determined to sail without my knowledge or consent.

Burbage had been able to tell me little of the surface reasons that prompted the Fields to join the expedition. Jaimie's health was not robust; his daughter had expressed the hope that a sea voyage, plus the salubrious climate of America, might restore his vigor. I will confess that I had listened to these tidings with but half an ear. Susanna, as I knew, had a will of her own, and an imagination to match it. Perhaps she really believed that a better life awaited her across the Ocean Sea. Or had she simply challenged me to give up Elvira and follow her—if I could prove myself worthy?

I could not answer that question now, nor could I blame her. In the Queen's own presence she had told me of her intention, and I had been too stupid to realize that she spoke the simple truth. Now, with my love on the high seas and my own departure delayed, I could only pace the deck of Raleigh's flagship and curse the foul weather that kept us in Plymouth.

Raleigh had gone up to London to put his affairs in order and to purchase extra victuals for the ships that remained at anchor. On his return to Plymouth, he had been grateful to me beyond all measure—so grateful that I had risked a full confession of my love for Susanna. He had promised to do all he could to insure her safety, once we had joined forces.

Beyond that, there was no way he could prevent me from eating out my heart.

Raleigh's voyage to Guiana, and his explorations of its mysteries, are part of England's history, written by his own hand. I will make no attempt to amplify the account in these pages. Nor will I discuss events in which I was not directly involved, save in passing.

Suffice it to say that we left Plymouth at last, in the teeth of a fresh gale. At the final moment I was transferred from Raleigh's flagship, the *Dragon*, to the *Lion's Whelp*. This stout vessel, with Captain Thomas Gross commanding, served as a rear guard, while we ghosted down the Spanish coast, to keep a weather eye for enemy topsails. Thereafter we pressed on for the Canaries and a route that would take us east by south, until we fetched the northeastern tip of the great island of Trinidad.

Save for the bad weather which plagues these latitudes in winter, our crossing proved uneventful. Our rigging was crippled by high seas before we could quite reach the Canaries, so that we were forced to heave to for repairs. The *Dragon* pressed on, eager to overtake the colonists' transport.

The *Lion's Whelp* had sailed under sealed orders, which could not be broken until we raised the Canaries. Captain Gross (a martinet who had been years in Raleigh's service) had shown me no special favor, though he knew I was Sir Walter's protégé. During our stormy passage I had stood my share of watches and gone aloft with the other hands. Now, however, I was summoned to his cabin for the breaking of the seals, a ceremony we performed behind locked doors, with only his mates in attendance.

Gross cursed long and earnestly when he had read through Raleigh's orders, then tossed the sheet to me. I read it with no particular surprise, since Sir Walter had already confided his plans in some detail.

Obviously he could not ignore the Queen's warning. Elizabeth had small love for an explorer who returned to London empty-handed. From what she had told me at Greenwich, she expected the *Dragon* to wallow home scupper-deep with gold —and was prepared, quite literally, to claim our leader's head if he disappointed her. Therefore Raleigh had no choice but to drive straight for Trinidad, with all the force at his command. At the same time, while the flotilla was at Plymouth, it had been necessary to circulate rumors confirming the forged patent I had given Quesada. Thus it was common gossip, from forecastle to quarter-deck, that our destination was Virginia. Captain Gross's burst of bad language showed that he had believed the rumors.

"I'm too old to fight the dons again," he roared. "Why can't we stake out a domain to the north and live there in peace?"

"If we move fast, it needn't come to fighting."

"There's a garrison on Trinidad—and a town of sorts. We'll be at loggerheads overnight."

"Not if we outnumber the garrison. They'll surrender without a shot." As I spoke I was wondering if Elvira had outsailed us; it seemed unlikely, in view of the Spanish fondness for procrastination. Even if she was now in Trinidad she could do us no harm, since she would have told her uncle that Virginia was Raleigh's goal.

"It's still a chancy business," said Gross. "Suppose we run afoul of the Spanish fleet?"

"Most of Philip's warships are refitting at Cádiz. I'll grant you it's a risk, sir—but that's how empires are founded. And Raleigh means to carve one in Guiana."

"Virginia is cooler—and safer."

"There's no Manoa in Virginia, and no Golden Ones."

"Tell me, MacManus," the captain said heavily, "have ye ever set foot in a rain forest?"

"Only in dreams, sir."

"Then neither have ye ridden out a hurricane on a lee shore —nor have ye kedged your way into this mad river they call the Orenoque. *I've* sailed that coast, and it's more gumbo than land. The only settlers it's fit for are ducks."

"In that case the colonists can remain on Trinidad while we go upstream."

"You're privy to Raleigh's thoughts, lad. Does he really intend to explore the river valley?"

"So he says—and I've no cause to doubt him."

"Nor do I, now I've read my orders," said Gross. "Don't mind an old man's jaw. I've howled before when I've sailed with Sir Walter, and done his bidding. Still, I wish the lady at Whitehall could see that land is worth more than gold."

I remembered my first meeting with Raleigh, when he had told me that the true riches of the New World had scarcely been touched. Perhaps, had I argued more convincingly, the Queen might have forgotten her ancient enemy for once and permitted us to sail straight for Virginia. Yet even while I pondered this lost opportunity, I could not keep down my excitement as I pictured the explorations that awaited us. Manoa, and the gilded men who inhabited it, might be purest fable—but they seemed more real with each new mile of westing.

"Perhaps we'll break ground in Virginia later," I said. "If Guiana is unfit for habitation, we've the authority to move our settlers north. Meanwhile we've time to track down a few Spaniards and find the source of their ingots."

"Be honest, MacManus," the Captain growled. "D'you credit these tales about golden men and a golden city?"

"Why not, if they'll make me rich?"

" 'Tis part of youth, I suppose—hoping that wealth will come easy as breathing. But I'll tell ye this, lad, with our voyage scarce begun. If there's really an El Dorado in that rain forest, Raleigh will find it. And if it's inhabited by golden men, he'll deliver 'em to London, shiny hides and all."

There were more oaths before he dismissed me, and more dire prophecies. I made no attempt to counter his arguments. If only for Susanna's sake, I would have been far easier in my mind if these boatloads of colonists had headed north, to debark outside the danger zone. And yet, for all his gloom, I could sense that our captain, like myself, had caught some of Raleigh's fire. Now that the expedition was openly labeled a treasure hunt, the whole ship seemed to come alive, as though master and crew alike shared the same excited heartbeat.

El Dorado seemed close indeed when the first flash of sunlight on a sea bird's wing told us we were nearing land. Days later, when a blue shadow to the west cut into the ocean's perfect round, it was almost near enough to touch.

Since our charts were none too accurate, we shortened sail that night and followed a cautious offshore tack, lest we blunder on a reef. When the wind shifted after sunset we could smell the land, a hot, fervent exhalation that stirred the pulses after our long weeks at sea. It was an exotic smell, with the cloying breath of dead vegetation at its heart—black and faintly sinister, like the night that boxed us.

At midnight rain came down in a devil's tattoo—then ended abruptly as the freshening breeze swept the clouds away and let in a vast panoply of stars. Even these constellations seemed nearer than the stars at home, and many were strange to me. For the first time I realized how alien this New World was. So far it had held no hint of welcome.

Morning brought a following breeze and a shining azure sweep of sea, broken here and there by the creaming of surf on a reef—which Gross told me was built from the ocean's floor by millions of tiny shellfish he called "coral." The reefs were few, giving us ample sea room for our careful approach to the land. A nearer view showed us that the blue masses we had seen against the sunset were distant mountains. From the water's edge, as far as the eye could reach, a dense jungle swept inland. It was a tangled mass, dark green and unbroken save for a sluggish stream or two that spewed into the sea in wide, silty aprons. This, I gathered, was the rain forest of which Captain Gross had spoken in such gloomy terms. I was beginning to appreciate the picture he had drawn.

All that morning, while the wind continued to favor us, we sailed as near to the ominous coast line as we dared. A school of porpoise kept pace with us, playfully diving and surging

just ahead of our bow. Above our masts a long file of ungain-
ly birds (which Pablo said were pelicans) flew in a geometric
formation. Now and again one of them would plummet to
snatch a fish from the crystal-clear sea. There was no other
sign of life about us. The sullen green land (as I saw on closer
view) belonged to the dawn of history. Only a veritable army,
bearing axes and cane knives, could have carved a foothold in
that mass of palm and liana.

"Clearly this is no fit habitation for man," I said to my Indian bodyguard. "Is it a fair sample of Trinidad?"

"No, señor. These swamps are vast indeed, but higher
ground lies beyond."

Pablo's information was not borne out that day, as we continued our cautious progress. The rain forest seemed never-
ending and the air grew more humid as the day advanced.
When the wind shifted once again to the land, it brought a
steaming mist in its wake, which soon congealed into a down-
pour that could only be described as a cloudburst. While the
deluge lasted, it was impossible to set a course, since the wind
had died to a whisper and the curtain of white water obscured
the sea beyond our bows.

Longboats went out from the ships. Until sunset, when the
rain died down at last and a sluggish breeze sprang up in the
west, we kedged the *Lion's Whelp* on her course, a backbreak-
ing task that left us drenched in sweat and eager for our ham-
mocks. Without that sinew-cracking effort, the ship would
have surely drifted inshore until she grounded in the pulpy
sludge that was neither sea nor land.

I had tumbled into my hammock at sunset, to sink into a
dreamless sleep, careless of other downpours that continued
to drench the ship all through the night. Toward morning I
was conscious that the rain had stopped and that the slow rise
and fall of our bowsprit had also ceased. It was only when I
opened my eyes fully that I realized we had dropped anchor
in a roadstead blazing with sunlight.

Pablo was waiting with a platter of hardtack and a tankard.
I rubbed the sleep from my eyes while I breakfasted and
stared in silent wonder at the flag of England, whipping
smartly in the breeze from a tall pole on the shore. We had
taken our mooring less than two hundred yards from land, in
a deep-scoured channel between two islets that offered a natural protection at the harbor mouth. The bay itself, an al-

most perfect circle, was a deep cobalt; it was ringed with a tawny beach and backed by high, parklike country studded with palm groves and deep with lush grasslands that swept westward toward a vista of jungly ridges.

At first glance I could barely make out the score of palm thatch huts in the nearest palm grove, so perfectly did their green roofs blend with the landscape. Then, as I saw the cook fire burning cheerfully before each dwelling and the good English yeomen who bustled at the task of getting breakfast, I knew that I was witnessing history in the making, the stake-out of the first English settlement on the shores of New Spain.

True, the little colony had no look of permanence. The huts seemed frail things indeed, on their sapling stilts—and the settlers, in their British homespuns, had a castaway air about them, despite the songs that traveled from fire to fire in the sunny morning. Yet the bay seemed a veritable paradise when contrasted with my dismal memory of yesterday: the knowledge that Susanna and her father must be somewhere in that palm grove was enough to stir me to action.

Had I considered only my own interests, I would have swum ashore to find her. Just in time, I remembered that I was one of Raleigh's lieutenants.

"When did we fetch this anchorage, Pablo?"

"Just after sunrise, señor," said the Indian. "It seems our charts were accurate after all." My bodyguard spoke these last words with a certain pride, since he had taken a large part in drawing the map that Captain Gross was using.

"Where will I find Sir Walter?"

"The people say he's already sailed on."

Delighted as I had been by the prospect before us, I had failed to look for other moorings in the harbor. Farther down the roadstead, the two transport vessels had been careened in shallow water. Shipwrights were working busily on their seams, or scraping their barnacled keels. There was no sign of the *Dragon*.

"Find me a longboat," I said. "We're going ashore as soon as I can get permission."

Captain Gross was at breakfast in his cabin, with a map of Trinidad before him. "Sit down, MacManus," he growled. "There's ale in that tankard."

"I've had my ration for the morning, sir."

"Have another. You may need it when you hear my news."

I poured a bumper of the rich Kentish brew and washed down the lump in my throat. "Has Sir Walter suffered a mishap?"

"Far from it. At the moment, I gather, he's trimming another Spaniard's beard."

I listened in astonishment to his tidings. The *Dragon* had entered this roadstead three days ahead of us. They had found the colonists' vessels and their convoy, a smaller ship called the *Firefly,* riding serenely at anchor, with exploring parties already in the upland savannas, and hunters butchering wild pigs on the beach. Raleigh had sent two dozen pikemen ashore at once to make sure that no hostiles (either Indian or Spaniard) had gathered on our flanks. When the explorers returned and reported the whole area uninhabited, he had beached the colonists and put them to work erecting huts and setting out such vegetable plantations as they required.

So rich were the natural resources of the country, and so plentiful the game, that a viable settlement had been established almost overnight. Could they survive the rainy season, Sir Walter and his captains assured themselves that this colony might well be permanent—providing it was spared the fevers so prevalent in this region, and remained immune from enemy attack.

It was to forestall the second possibility that our leader had set sail for Port-of-Spain, Trinidad's only settlement, built at the head of a deep bay on the western side of the island.

It was now three days since he had descended on Port-of-Spain. Captain Nathaniel Cross, who was his second-in-command and in charge at this moment, expected his speedy return. Raleigh's strategy, as always, was both daring and simple. He could scarce afford to linger on this coast with an enemy at his back. Even if Don Antonio de Berreo proved too cowardly to attack us directly, he could still dispatch a call for help to the more populous islands—like Margarita to the north—whose soldiery would far outnumber us. With luck on our side, and the element of surprise added, Raleigh had every hope of surrounding Port-of-Spain and capturing its garrison *in toto,* without excessive bloodletting.

If he encountered resistance he was prepared to put the place to the torch and wipe out its last effective, on the sound principle that dead Spaniards tell no tales. . . . Most desired of all, naturally, was the living person of Don Antonio de Berreo, since we could use him as a hostage if the need arose. Raleigh hoped, as well, to extract valuable information from the governor—perhaps even a map of the region to supplement the chart that Pablo had drawn from memory.

"What if Port-of-Spain is stronger than Sir Walter thinks?" I asked. "Our information is not too recent."

Captain Gross snorted like the sea lion he resembled. "One thing you can count on, lad; now that they've used up their *conquistadores,* Spain has shot her bolt here. Perhaps they'll hang on for another century or two; they've dug in deep. But I've sailed into Port-of-Spain myself, aboard a Dutch privateer, and I can tell you it's no more than a grease spot. Raleigh's invested it with a hundred men-at-arms. He could reduce it with half that number."

"Suppose we *do* overcome Port-of-Spain and burn it to the ground. Suppose we bring captives to this roadstead, with their governor in the van. What happens next?"

"Trinidad is ours——"

"Until word reaches Havana, or Hispaniola?"

"Are you questioning Raleigh's strategy, lad?"

"Not for myself at least," I assured him. "But when he recruited colonists Raleigh said nothing to them of going against the Spanish. Besides, I've a prospective wife somewhere in yonder palm grove——"

"So I've heard. What of it?"

"How long will she be safe from the dons?"

"Why not ask Raleigh?"

"You've sailed these waters, sir. How near are the Spanish? And have they the strength to destroy us?"

Gross studied me narrowly. "You're a braw lad, MacManus," he said. "And a smart one. So I'll give ye my opinion straight. Were I in your shoes I'd postpone my marriage plans."

"May I ask why, sir?"

"Because this is Raleigh's greatest gamble, and you're part of it. We must help him track down these Golden Ones—and bring their treasure to London. Until that's done, ye've no time to think of weddings."

"Perhaps you're right," I said.

"Look at it with his eyes. For years he's cooled his heels in the palace courtyard—drilling the Queen's guard while Essex entertains Her Majesty upstairs. This is his chance to restore himself to favor. If he succeeds, there's nothing the old girl won't give him. He can colonize Virginia if he likes, or mount a war against New Spain itself. If he fails he'll go under a deeper cloud—or straight to the block. And England's stake in this New World must await another explorer to redeem it."

"Why tell me this? D'you doubt my loyalty?"

"Not at all, lad. I'm only reminding ye that it's a poor time for thoughts of self. So far you've been his good-luck charm. Wherever Raleigh goes, there MacManus must go too."

Ashore at last, I paid my duty call on Captain Cross before going in search of Susanna and Jaimie. The beach commander was a busy man today, with a score of questions to settle. Eventually he paused long enough to give me an account of Raleigh's voyage from the Canaries. While still in sight of land, they had taken a Spaniard laden with firearms. Later they had forced a Flemish master to strike his colors and had lifted twenty butts of wine from his hold, along with other plunder. Several of the casks were still unbroached; the others had been a godsend for the colonists on the last long reach across the Ocean Sea.

My own immediate task, Cross told me, would be to assist in the caulking of the ships he had careened on the beach. Specifically, I was to take charge of a scouting party now making ready for a short voyage down the coast of Trinidad to seek out the great lake of pitch that lay just behind the shore. This oddity of nature (called *La Brea* by Spanish explorers) had bubbled away for centuries in its vast jungle cradle, like a true outpost of hell. Once we had located *La Brea*, we were to bring back pitch in sufficient quantity to make our hulls shipshape. Naturally I was instructed to keep a sharp eye for hostiles en route, whether white or red.

I found Jaimie Field puffing his pipe in the sandy yard of one of the more commodious huts. The former stage keeper at the Theatre seemed completely at home. From his mahogany-dark visage to the loose nankeen trousers, he was part and parcel of that sun-steeped palm glade. His knockabout abode could as well have been a setting at the Theatre; he would not have greeted me more cavalierly had I stepped across Shoreditch Road between cues.

"Welcome to New London, Master Shawn."

"Are you the Lord Mayor?"

"So I be, lad, in a manner of speaking—though 'tis not a formal election."

I glanced through the little settlement and recognized several of our former apprentices under their fledgling beards, hard at work on a storage hut nearby. On the bank of a rivulet that flowed through the heart of the grove, more of these young rakehells were on hands and knees, washing their clothes and shouting as they worked. Fellows such as these had come and gone at the Theatre, as restlessly as magpies in the spring. Apparently it had been child's play for Jaimie to enlist a goodly number for Raleigh's venture; enough, at any rate, to make him a leader of sorts ashore.

"A sultan in his seraglio could hardly look more comfortable," I said.

"As ye well know, Shawn, I'm a bit too old for harems—but I won't deny I've cottoned to this life from the first. Even when it rains Susanna and I are snug here. When it's fine, life comes more than halfway to meet us, with a horn of plenty in each hand." He gestured toward a small area of yams outside the grove and a stand of green plantains just beyond. "More fruit and tubers than any army could devour; fish for the seining in our harbor, and wild pig and deer by the droves in the brakes. Were it not for the dons, I'd say we'd blundered into the last Eden on earth—and Raleigh's already gone to spike *their* guns."

The estimate, I reflected, was somewhat on the rosy side, but I could understand Jaimie Field's ardor. A son of the London stews, he had swinked his living all through his boyhood, until a stroke of luck had brought him under Burbage's wing. Even at the Theatre, existence had been a hit-or-miss affair. I knew that he and Susanna had endured their share of hardship on the not infrequent occasions when politics or the fear of plague had forced the playhouse to close its doors. Now that he had blundered into this lush milieu, he could hardly be blamed for thinking that he held the future in his palm.

"I trust the voyage was a smooth one, Jaimie?"

"Smooth enough for good sailors like Puss. I'll confess I was sick as a dog from the day we left Plymouth. It's a price I'd gladly pay again for this safe harbor."

Let's hope you don't live to eat those words, I thought. "Do the others share your views?"

"We're city sparrows," he said. "Can you picture a happier adventure for a hundred waifs whose only food was the bitter bread of poverty?" His years in the Theatre had given Jaimie's language a certain florid turn. Now, to underline his words, he lifted one hand in benediction. Moses on the threshold of Canaan could hardly have been more benign.

"God grant that Sir Walter can make this New London permanent. I'd be content to end my days here."

"You might have informed me of your decision to join the venture," I told him.

He winked and laid a finger along his nose: it was our stage keeper's usual gesture when he refused to answer questions. " 'Tis a fair enough reproach, Shawn," he said. "And it's one that Puss herself should answer. You'll find her on the beach, seining for our supper."

My progress through the palm-thatch settlement was slowed considerably by friends from Shoreditch, who left their tasks a dozen times to shake my hand. When I gained the beach it seemed deserted, save for a few scuttling land crabs. Then, after I had rounded a densely wooded point to the south, I found Susanna, thigh-deep in the shallows, in the act of drawing a seine from water to land.

The hammering of my heart, at first view of her, seemed too great to be borne; until it slowed its beat I drew back a moment more into my jungle ambush, while I watched her empty the catch into a basket and prepare for a fresh cast. It seemed but natural that Susanna should be wearing the same apprentice's garb I remembered from our first meeting. Utterly intent on the task at hand, she was as oblivious of my presence as though the Ocean Sea still divided us. Whatever my Puss did, she did it with all her mind and heart—whether it was the recital of a scene of Will Shakespeare's, the seining of her father's supper, or the baiting of Shawn MacManus, the feckless Irelander who had strode into her life unasked.

Bewitched as I was, I could have gone on watching forever. In sober truth I was half afraid to break the spell, lest she turn into the vixen I remembered so painfully from our night in Greenwich. And yet, step by step, I found myself drawing ever nearer to the water's edge, as though my feet were braver than my mind. I was knee-deep in the bay before she turned and saw me: the best greeting I could offer was a strangled attempt to speak her name.

"You were long enough getting here," she said.

"You knew I'd come in time, Puss——"

"You great booby—why else would I cross half a world to wait for you?"

She had already cast the net aside; now she splashed through the shallows to meet me with both arms held out. The kiss of greeting she gave me, there on the New World's edge, was like stumbling on El Dorado unaware.

CHAPTER XIII

An Outpost of Hell

"SAY YOU love me," she ordered. "Say it again and again. I could listen forever, now I'm sure you mean it."

"I've loved you, Puss, from the moment we met in the Theatre."

"And that night in the sewing room?"

"What good is love, without desire to spark it? I'll ask no pardon for those kisses, Mistress Field. Remember, you gave back all you received."

"And even then you loved me?"

"Then more than ever. Enough to put you from me until I could give more than kisses in the dark."

We were seated on the beach, with the fronds of a great coconut palm above us. After the ecstasy of that first long embrace I knew that our communion was complete. Fool that I'd been in England, I had not seen that her love matched my own. Or that a woman in love will forgive her man most things when the love is returned.

"What did you wish to give me, Shawn?"

"Nothing less than the riches of the Golden Ones."

"It was yourself I wanted that night—not gold. And you left me for a Spanish doxy."

"So I did. I can tell you why now."

"I've already learned why, with Sir Walter's help."

"You didn't go to him?"

"I was aboard the *Dragon* before she left Plymouth," said

Susanna calmly. "And pray, why not, Master Irishman? As a colonist, I was already under his command. Besides, I needed his permission to marry you."

"You decided to marry me—before I'd even asked you?"

"I'd settled that much in my mind before I'd known you two days."

"Isn't it maidenly to let the man do the asking?"

"The asking, yes. Never the deciding."

"Why leave me unclaimed so long, if you'd marked me as your prize?"

"Don't value yourself too highly, Master Shawn," she cried, with the airy impudence I knew so well. "Remember, there was still unfinished business. The black-haired jade was one item. Another was your monkey's way on the social ladder."

"You told Sir Walter *that?*"

"Marriage is a serious step. It behooves a girl to do what she can before she undertakes it."

"What was his answer?"

"He gave us his blessing—but he forbade the match for the present. At least until you've returned from your exploring, with the gilded men as your captives."

I could hardly dispute Raleigh's decision. Since I was pledged to follow him, I must go on his terms—and he would want no lovesick bridegroom in his entourage. Nor was it fair to Puss to make her my wife today, when she might become my widow tomorrow.

"Do *you* believe in the Golden Ones?" I asked.

"I've given them no thought, Shawn. Being here when the *Lion's Whelp* dropped anchor was all I cared about."

"El Dorado must exist. Else how could I promise you its riches? I won't begin our marriage with a lie, Puss."

"We'll find it somehow, my dear. Perhaps where we least expect. The Golden Ones are the least of my worries. The Spanish jade was something else."

"Did Raleigh set your mind at rest there?"

"He explained that bedding her was part of his scheme to cozen her uncle."

"I trust you believed him."

"I believed him. I could have wished you'd found the task less agreeable."

I let out my fears in a sigh of pure relief. "What of my ways in society?"

"Sir Walter explained that too. How could you fail to play the ape, since you're his double?"

She was laughing now. I saw that her mirth, for once, was directed at herself. "I won't deny that I was jealous in London," she said. "Of the girl from Madrid and of Raleigh's hold on you. Women can be fools in love, no less than men."

"What more did Sir Walter say?"

"He offered to send me back."

"I hope you accepted."

"You should know me better, Shawn. If this New World suits your fancy, we've come here to stay. If not, we'll go back together. But I'll not budge until you've decided."

I had put the query only to ease my conscience—knowing in advance what she would answer. "Did you ask Sir Walter's permission to join our voyage to the Orenoque?" I demanded. "It wouldn't surprise me in the slightest."

Susanna rose from her place beneath the palm and tossed her head proudly. "I'd go with you if he'd take me. Since that's impossible, I'm having a foretaste of the journey today."

"How, Puss?"

"By guiding your party to the pitch lake. And you needn't put on that frown. Captain Cross has granted me the right."

"Since when did you qualify as a guide to Trinidad?"

"I can sail as well as any man," she said. "Only yesterday I followed the coast in a dinghy, with Jaimie and two apprentices as ballast. *La Brea* is scarce two leagues to the south. We can fetch it in an hour."

A blast on a hunter's horn (the agreed-on signal from Pablo that would bring me to the harbor's edge) drifted through the hot morning air. It was an odd sound in that tropic setting, recalling frosty winter moorlands and a ride to hounds. It reminded me how far we were from home and how vast was the *terra incognita* on whose verge we stood. And yet, with Susanna's hand in mine, it was easy to shake off the nameless shiver that swept over me.

The *Dragon* had brought a pinnace to Trinidad—a shallow-draft boat that is sometimes called a *gallego*, an ideal craft for exploring unknown waters. It had been partly dismantled for storing during the voyage, but for the past two days a picked crew had worked hard to prepare it for launching. Now it was dancing smartly in the breeze, waiting only the raising of its mainsail. The four-man crew stood by the sheets: Pablo himself was at the tiller and greeted us with the smartest of salutes as we waded out to board her. Susanna was handed overside with a cheer. I saw that she had long since made friends with these four sturdy yeomen and was accepted by them as their equal, despite her sex.

The breeze had been muted in the landlocked harbor. When we slipped under the stern of the *Lion's Whelp* and gained the open sea, the pinnace took a brisk wind on her quarter and bowled through the whitecaps with all her sail taut. At Susanna's direction we set our course due south, keeping well offshore and watching carefully for the coral outcrop that made these waters dangerous for larger craft than ours.

Once we had dropped our anchorage astern, the aspect of the island changed dramatically as the parklike savannas merged with the everlasting jungle. Save for the ribbon of beach, there was literally nothing to break the monotony of that livid green wall. Unfamiliar as I was with this forbidding landscape, I feared that we might sail past our destination—but my nose gave me ample warning of its presence, less than an hour after we had put to sea. The Thames' greatest shipyard, with a hundred bubbling caldrons of pitch, could scarce have breathed out a more noxious vapor.

Shortly thereafter we set a course that brought us close to land. The white sand of the beach had already begun to shade into brown: before we had sailed another mile the whole area was dark as Satan's doorsill. At Susanna's suggestion, Pablo put over his helm and drove the pinnace into the muddy surf until it grounded. We had already donned our boots in preparation for our journey inland. Carrying a dozen buckets among us, we stepped overside into a world that seemed painted in every degree of black, from jet to copper brown. Even the pebbles rolling in the backwash of the surf were balls of hardened pitch. A pool (formed by the receding tide) had pitch bulwarks, though the minnows swimming there, oddly enough, seemed unaffected.

A dozen ebony lappets oozed from the forest, like molasses spilling from a too-full pitcher. I tested the stuff with a spade, but it was too mixed with vegetation to be useful for calking.

"Can you cut a trail, Pablo?"

"I can try, señor," said the Indian, and unlimbered the

great cane knife at his belt, an example the sailors followed. With these *machetes* it was a simple matter to hack away the lianas and giant ferns that were the principal barriers to our progress—but so dense was their growth that we found ourselves moving at a snail's pace.

Stepping into the embrace of the jungle was like entering a steam bath, a green inferno exotic beyond my wildest visions. The myriad leaves (many of them broader than a man) shut out the sky instantly, making a translucent gloom that was more night than day. Here, sprouting from the tree trunks themselves, were great, tigerlike flowers that Susanna called orchids. Farther on were golden flowers shaped like a giant's trumpet, blossoms with beards of imperial purple, a burst of silvery bloom where the trees let in a patch of sky. This white avalanche (to which not even Pablo could assign a name) reflected the sun so brilliantly that it resembled a monster chandelier.

Snakes were everywhere, coiled in the trees, or slithering from our path. Some of these reptiles had strange, buttonlike tails, which gave off a shirring sound not unlike a child's top (we gave these creatures a wide berth, since I had read that their bite could be venomous). Moths, as huge as the bats they resembled, darted among the foliage, pursued here and there by golden-green birds, and parakeets with rainbow-hued wings scolded us from every branch. It was a scene to delight the artist, even as it gave one pause, for there was something revolting in this green opulence—and something faintly sinister too, though I could not give it a name.

A half hour's work with the cane knives brought us perhaps a quarter mile from the beach. The acrid reek of *La Brea* was stronger now, as though a dragon was couched in that green bed, breathing vaporously in its slumber. It was obvious that we must seek a more direct approach however, if we meant to fill our pitch buckets today—so we turned to the beach again and spread sail.

On this occasion, our luck improved. A mile to the south, we came upon a tiny bay, bordered by mangroves whose gnarled roots, exposed by the falling tide, proved to be covered with succulent oysters. As it was now the dinner hour, we paused to partake of this ready-made repast, while Pablo scouted a path of sorts, formed by the bed of a watercourse that serpentined into the forest in the general direction we wished to follow. An hour later, when we had rested after eating (your English sailor, ashore in the tropics, falls readily into the Spanish habit of the siesta), we followed this stream in cautious single file.

It was muddy going at first, and the sluggish current was hip-deep in places. Here and there we disturbed the repose of those giant saurians which the Spaniards call *lagartos* and the English "crocodiles." The loathsome, scaly creatures seemed to resent our presence and greeted us with a great welter of tail-lashing and gaping jaws before they waddled from view. Had we not approached in such numbers, I suspected they might have attacked us outright.

After we had struggled onward for perhaps a mile, the jungle began to thin and it was possible to see beyond the banks. The stream now dwindled to a rill—and Susanna, whom I had carried pickaback, was able to walk again. For the second time we could sense the presence of the great pitch lake, though it was not yet in view. The bed of the watercourse was ink-dark and spongy to the footfall, and the land about it, as far as the eye could reach, resembled nothing so much as an English fen.

Another hundred yards and the stream ended in an oil-slick pool. We circled it with care (lest the bog turn to quicksand) and topped a slight rise beyond, to discover it was the containing wall of *La Brea*.

I will confess a certain disillusion at my first view of the Lake of Pitch, which travelers have since described (with more fervor than accuracy) as one of the world's wonders. I could hardly say what I had expected—a maelstrom of boiling tar, perhaps, like a vent from Avernus, or a jet-black sea too vast to measure. What I saw was a circular pool (perhaps a hundred acres in extent) on which the sun splintered in iridescent rays and from which an acrid stink rose skyward. Blacker than perdition for the most part, it was cinnamon brown in spots and chrome yellow in others. A few islets dotted its surface and a magnificent stand of palm trees seemed to sprout from the pitch itself on the western shore.

Gingerly we ventured to its edge—and then (with our hands joined) moved out to its surface. I had expected the pitch to be too hot to touch: actually we could just sense its inner heat through our boot soles, so thick was the congealed surface. Perhaps the best way to picture that surface is to compare it to a thousand giant mushrooms, some a good fifty yards across, all of them crushed together in grotesque deformity. Here and there, viscous liquid bubbled ominously beneath their domes, keeping the whole mass in restless motion. So far as I could judge, there was a definite boiling and roiling just below that oddly crusted surface, from heaven knew what infernal source. This mysterious activity was violent enough to erupt in sticky layers, which hardened rapidly in the open air. As this process continued, it was sufficient to thrust the old mushrooms from view, perhaps even to make them molten once again.

Our sailors, with Pablo in the van, set to work collecting the hardened pitch. While this went forward, Susanna and I ventured to the far side of the lake, where the caldronlike bubbling seemed most pronounced. Here the fumes were all but overpowering, with a definite reek of sulphur, proving my assumption that this was, indeed, an outpost of hell. With each step the footing grew more treacherous, until our boots sank ankle-deep. I persevered, since I knew that Raleigh would wish a complete report on this bizarre phenomenon. Then, as I felt Susanna's fingers grow cold in mine, I began to retrace our footsteps.

At our return we found the last bucket loaded and our party anxious to depart. Even in bright daylight, the place had a forlorn air; now that the afternoon rain clouds were gathering, it seemed truly accursed of God and man. Susanna was shivering when we waded into the stream again. She had mounted my back for the second time, and it pleased me mightily to feel her trembling ease away after I had served a few moments as her beast of burden. It was the first time in our relationship that she had taken heart from my strength. I hoped it would not be the last.

"Sorry you came?" I asked.

"I'm *glad*, Shawn—now it's over."

"Not many men have visited that devil's dell and lived to tell the story," I said. "I'll venture you're the only woman."

"It wasn't the Lake of Pitch I feared. It was the jungle we fought through that first hour. There was something *evil* about it, as though it was an enemy too strong to conquer. Didn't you feel the threat?"

I nodded solemnly, glad she could not see my face. *Threat,* I reflected, was only part of it; a threat can be fought, once its size is measured. But the rain forest of this region was old as time and contemptuous of man. It would resist us to the end. If ramparts like these guarded El Dorado, our task was formidable indeed.

"At least I know what you'll be facing," said Susanna. "It'll be comfort of a sort."

"How so, Puss?"

"Nothing is worse than the unknown," she said quietly, and rested her cheek against mine, as I dodged a branch that hung low above the stream. "Now we've fought through this forest together, I'll sleep better until your return."

"Pablo says there's a water route to Manoa."

"If that's true, why has it remained undiscovered?"

"Maybe because of the laziness of the dons—or their cowardice."

"So you'll cling to your dream to the end."

"Would you have me desert Raleigh and take you back to London? Or turn me into Burbage's stage keeper to support you?"

"It would content me beyond measure, Shawn. But I know that's too much to ask of any husband, when El Dorado beckons."

We said no more after we entered the last lap of our tramp to the beach. In sober truth, the sweltering journey to *La Brea* had brought us to the point of exhaustion. The return voyage revived our spirits, thanks to the tonic offshore breeze that usually rises in these latitudes with the approach of sunset. Entering the harbor on a last long tack, we trolled out a sailor's chantey, with Susanna's clear soprano carrying the air—a song that changed to a cheer when we saw that our flagship had dropped anchor in our absence.

The *Dragon* made a brave silhouette against the declining day as she rose at her mooring near the *Lion's Whelp*. Longboats were plying between the two vessels—and even at that distance, I could see that there were strangers on the deck of Raleigh's ship. The sight cheered us mightily, since it probably meant the raid had been successful. Not that I had ever doubted the prowess of so shrewd a warrior as Sir Walter, particularly with the element of surprise in his favor—but it lifted a weight from my mind to catch the smell of victory in the air.

So great was our elation, we sailed once around the *Dragon* in triumph before we set a course for the beach. The rails were thronged with men-at-arms awaiting shore leave. They echoed our cheers to the last man, though Raleigh himself did not deign to appear. With an arm about Susanna, I stood in the bow to salute our colors while we came about. Then, reminding myself of the unfinished tasks before us, I ordered Pablo to take us to the beach, where we furled the mainsail and unloaded our precious cargo.

The bay was filled with reflected sunlight when I kissed Susanna good-by and commandeered a skiff. As we approached the *Dragon* with the westering sun behind us, I had a clear view of the ship and the three figures at the taffrail who were clearly prisoners of war, since a pair of midshipmen stood guard at the stair that led to the waist. I learned later that these hostages (for they were just that) had been given the captain's own quarters as a mark of courtesy. This was the hour when they were permitted to take the air under guard, as they were doing now on the narrow quarter-deck.

Two of the three faces that looked down at me were already familiar—one of them, indeed, was far too well known for my peace of mind. Elvira Quesada was studying me with icy reserve. Too late, I realized that she must have spied me in the pinnace, with an arm about Susanna. At her side was Don Felipe de Vera, aloof and faintly quizzical, his lips twisted into a smile that was half well-bred sneer. The third figure at the rail was a portly gentleman with white hair and melancholy dark eyes under a cocked hatbrim. This (as I would discover) was no less a personage than Don Antonio de Berreo, the governor of Trinidad and Raleigh's chief prize in his raid on Port-of-Spain.

I saluted them courteously while the longboat glided toward the boarding ladder. Elvira continued to look through me. De Vera turned aside, with one of those urbane shrugs a coxcomb so often assumes when he faces a situation beyond his ken. Only the *gobernador* of Trinidad (who governed no longer) lifted one hand in a tired acknowledgment of my salute before the bulky waist of the flagship hid him from view.

The midships area of the *Dragon* was a holystoned sweep of planking where it was Raleigh's custom to hold daily musters at sea. Tonight the crew was at mess; most of the men-at-arms were enjoying their first shore leave. The deck was deserted save for Raleigh's orderly (who stood guard at the chartroom door) and the midshipmen at the quarter-deck stair.

At the head of the boarding ladder I hesitated, with one leg still hugging the rail. Judging by his orderly's presence, our leader was at work within, either in conclave with his captains or poring over his maps. I had no wish to force myself upon him if he was deep in a brown study. Indeed, having discovered the identity of a certain prisoner now on the quarterdeck, there was no place in the New World I had less wish to visit than the *Dragon.* And yet—now that I had locked glances with Elvira—I had come too far to retreat.

I straddled the rail a moment more, while Pablo added our skiff to the nest of longboats that clustered about the boarding ladder. Then, bracing both shoulders, I stepped down to the midships of the *Dragon.* On the deck above, Elvira had moved to the rail, until she stood directly over me. I saw, with a certain relief, that her companions had withdrawn to the quarters they shared, leaving her to face me alone.

I swept off the sailor's cap I was wearing in a deep bow. She responded with an inclination of her head, as though she admitted my presence for the first time. There was nothing in her dress or bearing to suggest the captive. Save for its small panniers, and the lightness of a material suited to the tropics, her traveling gown was of modish cut. So was the light cloak she had tossed about her shoulders, and the straw bonnet that shaded her milk-white skin, as is the fashion with your Spanish beauty everywhere. I was only too aware of the contrast between us—I in brine-soaked pantaloons and naked to the waist, she with her all but regal bearing, and the obvious advantage of looking down on me. I bowed my head without speaking. Somehow I felt that she had earned this moment of aloof withdrawal.

"Come nearer, Señor Shawn," she murmured in Spanish. "I've a *regalo,* just for you."

"A *gift,* señorita?"

"Come nearer. Aren't you even curious?"

Instinct kept me where I was, even as the siren beckoned. It is all that saved my life. Already she must have realized she could not entice me. The guards, unaware of the meaning of our exchange, continued to face me with arms folded on their drawn cutlasses. They could not see the torment in her eyes —or the silken flash of thigh when she whipped aside a pannier and plucked out the knife in her garter.

Pablo, who had just clambered up to join me, guessed Elvira's purpose and flung himself between us. His leap jolted me aside, protecting my heart and other vital organs. I still towered a head above him, and my throat was target enough. Had she been able to fling the knife in the same fluent sweep that lifted it from her garter, Elvira would have pinned my gizzard to the mast. Thanks to Pablo, the best she could do was balance it on one palm and hurl it point-blank.

I had but a second's respite, but it gave me time to gauge the throw and to swivel aside when it came. The knife, taut as a tuning fork, plucked a single high note from the air as it sank deep in the deck. For an instant more, Elvira seemed to hang above me, and I could have sworn that her hair lifted from her scalp like Medusa's. The guards (they were both young lunkheads) turned at last to the quarterdeck stair, but I held them in their places with a single barked command.

"Easy, lads," I said. " 'Twas but a court dagger I loaned the lady in England. As you see, she's returned it promptly."

Elvira hardly waited for my words before she fled to her cabin and slammed the door behind her. My knees shook a bit as my fingers closed on Pablo's arm in a gesture of thanks. Then, plucking the knife from the deck, I made a great show of placing it in my belt before I turned to the chartroom and demanded an audience with Raleigh.

CHAPTER XIV

Into the Unknown

RALEIGH PLAYED with the dagger as we talked. There was a great stack of notes on his table, scrawled in his familiar spidery hand. Now and again he turned them over and seemed to read at random. As I have said, his was a brain that worked on many levels. Tonight he was plotting his assault on El Dorado, even as another part of his mind refreshed itself with my tragicomic brush with eternity.

"Did she really mean to kill you?"

"I'm sure of it."

My mentor stroked his beard. I knew that his fingers

masked a smile. "She loves you, lad—there's no avoiding that. I knew it from the first talk we had."

"You've discussed me, sir?"

"There was no need. I read it in her voice when she asked news of you. Waste no pity on her. As our friend Will might say, she's hoist with her own petard. Or should we say well roasted in the fire she's used to burn so many others?" He tossed me the dagger. "Keep this, Shawn, as a reminder. When you've enjoyed a woman's favors—and desire her no longer—it's best to confess the fact. Even though she screams like a hellcat, it's over sooner."

"This time I hadn't the courage."

"I feared as much: that's why I told her all I could, after we'd made her our prisoner. Naturally I took the blame for every trick you played in London. It did nothing to cool the lady's rage."

I kept my own solemn look with an effort. Now that the danger was behind me, I had a strange urge to laugh aloud. True, I had lied when I had pretended to sue for Elvira's hand, but Elvira herself had begun our love duel with a lie when she first climbed into my bed. Nor could I regret that I had kept up the pretense to the end. Had Quesada suspected it *was* a game, we would not be snugly at anchor here, with a thousand leagues between us and King Philip's ships of war. . . . Or so I reasoned, while Raleigh's quiet voice went on.

He had much to tell me since our last meeting, and he told it tersely, as always, without wasting breath.

The sack of Port-of-Spain, I gathered, had relied on daring as well as surprise. Certainly the dons had been thunderstruck when his men-at-arms stormed in by land and sea. Your Spaniard will make war in the grand manner when he outnumbers you. When the odds are even he will usually take to his redoubt and wait out your siege. In this case, with his outer defenses breached, he had fought stubbornly. The hunt had spread from house to house in the tiny seaport town. Before it was over, the capture of Port-of-Spain had developed into what the French call *guerre à outrance,* or war to the end.

Few prisoners had been taken in the bitter fighting. The dons, expecting no quarter, had preferred swift death to surrender. Some had escaped into the jungle but in the end, when only the stockade remained to them (and the attackers had set it afire with pitch arrows), Don Antonio de Berreo had sent his aide to parley. Port-of-Spain was now reduced to ashes. Don Felipe de Vera, reading the portents accurately, had chosen capitulation.

Both De Berreo and his aide had given their paroles when they surrendered their swords. Save for the governor's niece, and a few survivors in the redoubt, Raleigh had brought back no other hostages. Elvira's capture had been pure bad fortune. Had the attack been mounted a day later, she would have been safely en route to Margarita, the principal Spanish settlement to the northwest—a genuine strong point in Philip's New World empire, of which Port-of-Spain had been only a feeble outpost.

I had been studying the maps while Raleigh told his story: now, with a finger on the roadstead of Margarita, I asked my first question.

"We're masters of Trinidad at this moment," I said. "The whole Guiana coast is open. What if its governor sends a punitive expedition?"

"Rest easy on that score, Shawn. Margarita has the arms and the men, but there are no ships at this season. Nor will they have transport until the next galleon calls from the isthmus. Meanwhile, if all goes well, I'll have staked out our claim to Manoa and the seven cities of gold."

"Seven, sir?"

"The charts agree. The land of the Golden Ones comprises not one city but seven."

I looked into his eyes, not liking the gleam I found in their depths. "Has anyone *really* seen El Dorado, sir?"

"A nephew of Pablo's journeyed there. He has since been put to death. But Pablo drew a map from the boy's memories."

"You'd risk our lives on an Indian's memory?"

"Why not—when his map coincides with the one we took at Port-of-Spain?"

I had a sharp recollection of an afternoon among the box hedges at Whitehall—and Elvira's story of a map in her uncle's possession. Raleigh, I gathered, had lost little time in forcing its surrender.

"May I see these maps, sir?"

"Of course, lad."

As he spoke, Raleigh glanced toward the door, which had stood open during our interview. After I had risen to close it he spread two charts for my inspection. One—which Pablo had drawn for us in London—was familiar enough. Amazingly detailed (when I remembered that it had been sketched in by an aborigine), it showed the delta of the Orenoque, the contours of the river valley, and the feeder stream—the Caroni—which led direct to Manoa, pictured in an appropriate sunburst at our journey's end.

The other map (which had been part of our booty at Port-of-Spain) was surprisingly similar, though the skill of the professional cartographer was now evident.

Significantly, both maps ended at the headwaters of the Caroni, with no exact indication of the relationship of Manoa to the banks of that river—though the route thither seemed plain as a coaching road in England.

"Can we set a course by these, sir?" I asked, trying to mask my doubts.

"With Pablo and De Vera to guide us? Why not?"

"Did you say *De Vera?*"

"I did, Shawn. This is a chart he inherited from his kinsman, Bartolomeo de Vera—who saw Manoa with his own eyes."

In London I had heard of Bartolomeo de Vera, a reckless explorer who had dared to make the Orenoque journey with only Indians as guides. This De Vera (so the story ran) had a gift of tongues—and a genius rare among the dons for making friends of the caciques along that river. What was more remarkable, he had returned to publish the tale of his journey, though the chart that gave it meaning had remained a family heirloom.

Was it possible that the map Elvira had mentioned at Whitehall and this carefully drawn chart were one and the same? The map had been in her uncle's possession, but that, too, was logical enough. Recalling my brief glimpse of De Vera at the Queen's levee, I could hardly doubt that he was among her suitors. Probably he had offered the map to cement the marriage settlement—with the understanding that he would share in any discoveries that resulted.

"May I ask how this chart came into your possession, sir?"

"It was taken at Port-of-Spain, along with other papers."

"But it belongs to De Vera?"

"It bears his signature as well as his kinsman's. The governor feels it is worthless. De Vera tells another story."

"Which do you believe, sir?"

"De Vera's map verified what we already knew," said Raleigh.

"You're confident, then, it isn't trickery?"

"Talk to him, and see for yourself." Raleigh was already on his feet, shouting for his orderly.

I made no protest as the prisoner was brought to the chartroom. How could I, when I could already read our leader's intentions? De Vera's entrance only confirmed my first impression, which had been unfavorable enough. I had remembered him from Whitehall as a brash fellow, albeit a handsome one. Save for the fact that he wore no side arms, he was still the classic popinjay as he took the chair that Raleigh offered.

My mentor began the interrogation, thrusting the chart before him and spreading his hands, as though inviting a frank response.

"This *is* the famous map, señor?"

"Of course, *jefe.*" The man's civil answer was startling enough. So was the guileless look he offered Raleigh.

"Why does the governor of Trinidad say it's worthless?"

"Don Antonio thinks El Dorado is a myth," said the other. "Unfortunately, he has been among the seekers. It happened when he first came here; he took the wrong path and just escaped with his life. The experience has clouded his views of Guiana."

"Did he use your map?" I asked.

"No, Master MacManus. I was not then in his service."

"You've offered to act as our guide," I said. "How can we know that the offer is genuine?"

He shrugged, as only a Spaniard can. "Take me with you when you ascend the Orenoque. I'll share the dangers."

"We already have a guide."

"Match my knowledge with his. You'll see who serves you best."

"What are your terms?"

"A fair share of the gold," said De Vera blandly. "And ransom for myself and Doña Elvira."

I read the hate in his eyes and spoke quickly. "Why include the lady?"

"We plan to marry, if I can insure our safe return to Madrid."

"It will be arranged," said Raleigh.

"What will Don Antonio say to this?" I demanded.

"As a prisoner, I take orders from my jailer," said the Spaniard, with a lupine grin I liked even less than his civility. "Don Antonio de Berreo is a servant of the Crown, and a devoted one. As for me—I am for De Vera."

"We already have your kinsman's map," I said, with an eye on Raleigh. "We've a native guide we can trust. What's to prevent us from voyaging into Guiana and giving you nothing?"

"Sir Walter will answer—I hope."

Raleigh spoke up as promptly as though the Spaniard had cued him in advance. Bartolomeo de Vera, I gathered, had been a diligent explorer when he ascended the Caroni. On his return he had paused at Morequito, a native village that stood near the juncture of that river with the Orenoque. Here he had signed treaties that would provide adequate transport on his return, barges for the gold he meant to take back to Spain, and a fleet of those light-draft, skin-and-willow craft the dons call *canoas*.

Intending to return with miners and other artisans, the elder De Vera had perished in a hurricane when he was en route to Madrid. Fortunately a copy of his map had remained in the family archives. It was this map that Felipe de Vera had offered the governor of Trinidad, as an earnest of his intentions toward the governor's niece—and proof of his determination to finish what his kinsman had begun. Our strike at Port-of-Spain had written finis to that plan.

Listening to this smoothly told story, I could understand Raleigh's interest. Without Pablo's map, it could easily pass for moonshine. As things stood, we might find the Spaniard useful. His price was modest. With Pablo as our bellwether, we could rule out treachery. Finally, the magic of the De Vera name might smooth our journey, once we reached Morequito.

It had seemed odd that the upper reaches of the Orenoque had been well drawn on both maps, whereas the mouth was barely sketched. Glib as always, De Vera explained that the river had many outlets, all of them contained in a huge delta. At this season the delta was badly silted, so that only shallow-draft boats could enter. The first part of our journey might therefore prove the most hazardous, since the gulf that separated Trinidad and the mainland was tempestuous, roiled, as it was, by the outpourings of the river and racked by constant squalls.

Once he had convinced himself that De Vera would be an asset to our expedition—and once I had grudgingly agreed—Raleigh pushed through the preliminaries with the utmost speed. A meeting of the captains was held that same night; the vote to explore Guiana forthwith was unanimous.

Gross was named second-in-command, after he had won the toss among the captains. Nathaniel Cross (another crony of Sir Walter's) was elected to remain at the anchorage, where he would command the flotilla and give orders to those ashore. Seventy men-at-arms, all volunteers, were to accompany our strike for the interior. Raleigh planned to take his own company on the pinnace and to divide the others among every longboat that could bear sail. These (plus the barges that awaited us at Morequito) would be sufficient to ferry the treasures of Manoa to the sea. My mentor planned to bring back no more than a modest gleaning from this venture—enough to convince the Queen that the region was worthy of settlement.

Now that it was almost spring, we knew that we must return before freshets made the rivers dangerous. Two days were needed to pitch the boats, load them with provisions, and prepare our arms. Every minute of my time was occupied. When the day of our departure dawned I was allowed but the briefest of shore leaves to bid Susanna and Jaimie Field farewell.

Her final kiss was warm on my lips when I stepped aboard the pinnace. Somehow I had thought this voyage of discovery would have its own drama—a salvo from the *Dragon*, perhaps, or a cheer from the lads we had left behind. But Raleigh had ordered that we slip out quietly, lest the dons from Margarita, even now, might be spying on our activities. For this reason, we had left the anchorage in the first flush of dawn. Save for Susanna and her father, hardly a dozen folk were up to wish us well. . . . At least I could rejoice that Elvira's cabin on the flagship was shuttered. Raleigh had told me that both she and her uncle would be confined there during our absence.

The sea was glassy green, with an east wind. Once we had cleared Trinidad we could make out the blue-gray mass of the mainland and were inclined to discount the gloomy picture both Don Antonio and his aide had drawn of the crossing. We had cause to revise that estimate in the next few hours. With the wind at our backs (blowing both the sea and the tide toward the wide delta of the Orenoque), and the outpourings of the river clashing with that watery movement in mid-sea, we soon found ourselves tossed on the quarreling waves like so many chips.

All that afternoon it was touch and go whether we would capsize, or, what was worse, dash ourselves to pieces against the mainland. Fortunately for us, each longboat was captained by an old sea dog; eventually we rode out the chop— with a few narrow escapes as the boats threatened to broach to between the crests. Just before darkness fell, we won our way to a small roadstead, which Raleigh identified from our charts as the Bay of Guanipa.

The narrow channel, formed by the southwestern point of Trinidad and the jut of the mainland, has been well named by the Spaniards—the *Boca de la Sierpe,* or Serpent's Mouth. The charts (vague as they were) suggested that the main mouth of the Orenoque emptied into the sea at this point, but we had no intention of entering it, even if we could have marked the channel in the steamy haze of evening. Instead, we meant to traverse the delta by one of its westerly entrances and come upon the main channel well above its junction with the sea, where we could force our way upstream with oars.

Exhausted as we were, and wet to the skin from the driving spray, we were glad to make a frugal supper on biscuit and dried beef before we collapsed in the bottoms of our craft to catch such sleep as we could. We lit no fires that night, nor did we venture to set foot on shore—if that boggy morass could be dignified with such a name.

The morning, blazing with flawless sunlight, revived our spirits somewhat; so did the ration of Flemish wine that Raleigh ordered passed among the boats. With shortened sail, and a leadsman in each bow, we set out along that spongy coast seeking a stream that would prove a navigable strait to the Orenoque.

Pablo had often hunted and fished this coast, but such landmarks as he could remember were no longer useful. The river, probing at its delta with a hundred tongues, was constantly opening and closing new channels. Many of these, with aprons of silt at their mouths, could not even be approached. Others (which we investigated gingerly with a pilot boat while the remainder of the flotilla stood prudently offshore) seemed promising from the sea, then proved to be no more than sloughs.

Our game of hide-and-seek with the river proved discouraging indeed. For three sun-blistered days we continued to follow false trails, only to turn back each time. On the fourth day our patience was rewarded when we blundered into what seemed another slough—until we tested its current with our sweeps. Judging by the steady pulse of the water, this was indeed part of the Orenoque; whether or not we could follow it to the confluence with the parent stream remained to be seen.

It was necessary, in this narrow channel, to drop all sail and work with the oars. At Raleigh's order, Pablo and I transferred to one of our river barges, a flat-bottomed vessel ideally suited to scouting these waters. Manned as it was by eight oarsmen, we were soon well in the lead and setting a lusty pace for our comrades. With each driving stroke we could feel ourselves nearer to our first great objective. I had already opened my mouth to troll out the first measures of a barcarole when I spied a flash of color ahead, which Pablo identified as the prow of a *canoa,* with three naked aborigines at the paddles.

Rowing eight to three, it was a simple matter to draw abreast of the savages; in another moment we had grappled their gunwale. So frightened were the natives, I feared they might cast themselves into the river. As Pablo translated their chatter, I found that they were restrained only by their fear of the crocodiles that swarmed on the nearby mud flats.

Fortunately they lost their panic when we showed no intention of molesting them—and accepted our gifts of beads and other baubles. With Pablo as our interpreter, we easily persuaded them to lead us to their village, a congeries of wattled huts upstream.

These people, we learned, were the Ciawani, a branch of the Tivitivas, the dominant tribe of the coastal regions. We did not venture to set foot on the shore, though I ordered our rowers to nuzzle the bank to facilitate the rituals of barter. The Ciawani spokesman was a white-haired ancient who was evidently their headman, though he was nude as the others and gave off the same goatlike stink.

The river we had penetrated, he said, was a true branch of the Orenoque—though it was unnamed on our maps. (Raleigh christened it the Red Cross, since we were obviously the first white men to penetrate its mysteries.) Three days' journey upstream, according to our informant, it joined with a far larger branch, the Amaná, which led in turn to the Orenoque. All of these streams had been swollen by heavy rains—though the true rainy season was some weeks distant. Even so, we could foresee a hard fight with the current once we pushed beyond tidewater.

Since at the time of the rains all these lowlands are flooded, with the exception of a few hillocks, the Ciawani raised their homes on monstrous stilts, and, in some cases, lodged them in the treetops themselves, as though they were, in sober fact, a species of bird life. The sight was a graphic reminder of what we must expect, should we be trapped upstream. It was my suggestion (which both Gross and De Vera supported) that we engage this headman as our guide. Even a day's rowing might make the difference between triumph and disaster, and this ancient Indian, despite his scrofulous exterior, had the air of a water rat who was thoroughly of his element.

When Raleigh had assented to this suggestion we found it a surprisingly easy matter to strike a bargain—though he insisted that two of his favorite wives accompany him, and every offspring of these unions old enough to wield a paddle. Four *canoas* were added to our fleet, to accommodate these folk, and a fifth was purchased outright for Pablo, De Vera, and myself, that we might continue our practice of scouting the water lanes. In addition, we acquired a stock of food from the Ciawani to augment our own fast-dwindling supplies—and, in considerably higher spirits, resumed our journey that same afternoon.

Though our *pourparlers* had been long, we had been careful to label ourselves simple explorers, lest word of our goal precede us. Pablo had explained the strange method by which the Indians are able to send messages across great distances. Long before we turned the first bend in the Red Cross River we could hear the Ciawani drums begin their throbbing, and picked up the answer in the maze ahead. Innocent though we hoped the message was, we could not quite suppress our dread. Those drums seemed to speak out of a vanished time.

As we proceeded, I was at great pains to correct the charts, in the light of what our newest guide had told us (his name was a thing of many syllables, beyond our English tongue, so we ended by calling him Tivi). Subsequent voyagers have confirmed our pioneer estimate, namely, that the Orenoque falls into the sea through nine branches to the north of its main channel and to the south through seven. This incredible, sprawling delta was a full hundred leagues in extent, and composed of many islands, some of them mere palm tufts, others fully as large as the Isle of Wight. It had been only by the rarest good fortune that we had blundered into one of these sixteen branches—and the acquisition of Tivi as our pilot was all that kept us in that channel in the days that followed.

Three days later we were still wallowing up that same endless brown stream and mingling curses with our prayers.

By this time we were beyond the tidal reach, when it had been possible to ride the flood with only a token exertion of our oars, to fish and hunt at the ebb, and then to push on with the return of the ocean's restless pulse. Now we matched our muscles against the remorseless river, straining at the oarlocks until our sinews cracked and our sweat-drenched bodies yearned for the sunset that would bring its numbed repose.

Twice, the pinnace grounded on sand bars; when we reached the Amaná it was decided to moor her in the nearest cove, since the thrust of the current in the wider stream made it impossible to drive so large a craft farther. Had we been able, we would have sailed her upstream, but the Amaná was too thickly spaced with sand bars to make tacking possible even if the towering rain forest had not shut out more than the merest whisper of a breeze.

According to Captain Gross (who had brought his navigating instruments from the *Lion's Whelp*), we were little more than five degrees north of the equator, so that the sun beat down upon that green-brown water mirror from its rising to its setting. With each mile, it seemed, the heat grew more oppressive. We had long since learned to welcome the occasional rain squalls as merciful respites and rowed into their teeth with our parched gullets open to their pelting.

Such rain as we had encountered, so far, was of brief duration. When the heavens opened wide we knew that it would be impossible to venture farther. Worst of all, we found that our supplies were already running low, thanks to the high percentage of spoilage in that climate. It was a difficult situation, and only the mighty example that Raleigh set kept the grumbling down to a murmur. For my part, I had long since despaired of seeing Morequito, or even the confluence of the Amaná and the Orenoque. Here, Tivi assured us, we could obtain an abundance of food, as well as sailing *canoas* aplenty for our assault on the mother river.

On the sixth day, when the remorseless sun was at its zenith, we fetched a lightning-blasted tree which Tivi recognized as a final marker—swearing by all his gods that the Orenoque was no more than another league distant. Six hours later, with nightfall imminent, there was still no break in the rain forest, and even Raleigh was half willing to hang our pilot for what seemed a gross betrayal. Then, as the sunset spread its angry red patina on the stream, we rounded yet another bend and found ourselves opposite an Indian village of over a hundred huts, rising like grotesque land birds from the muddy shore.

Straight ahead, where the current spouted on a sand bar in angry surf, was a vast inland sea, shining with the reflected glory of the sunset and pulsing with a turbid life of its own. It was only when I narrowed my eyes and took a second, longer look that I made out the blue-black line of the southern bank.

"Esta el río Orenoque, señor," said Pablo, as he wiped the sweat from his brow. Then, spinning his paddle, he set the *canoa* driving for the village.

Sunset had blotted the Orenoque before we could beach our craft, and cook fires were winking before the huts when the last of our tired flotilla stepped ashore. The natives (who had thronged to the river's edge on our arrival) seemed diffident at first, and the children clung to their mothers' kirtles and squealed in terror. We understood why when we regarded one another. Most of us had long since peeled to the buff for coolness' sake; we had plastered our bodies with river mud to keep off the insects. Even to these primitive folk, we must have seemed visitors from another planet.

Raleigh (who alone amongst us had managed to keep his bandbox elegance) stepped forward with his hand up, palm outward. Pablo, with a white square of cloth nailed to a paddle, completed the gesture of peace. We soon learned that Tivi's promise had been accurate; there was bread and meat in abundance here, as well as gallon gourds of a potent brew which these people extract from the juice of the palm heart. As for transport, there were sailing *canoas* by the dozen. This particular tribe—called the Arwacas—dwelt almost entirely along the Orenoque itself, and excelled in the construction of such craft.

Tired though I was, I observed that we were vastly outnumbered, and could not help but wonder what might have occurred had these simple people decided to take over our boats and possessions outright and slay us in the bargain. However, they seemed friendly enough once they had helped us to wash at the river's edge, and assured themselves that our white skins had the same texture as their own. Indeed, I could see that friendliness had passed the bounds of decorum in several instances, for the younger, hardier members of our company had already begun to sport with the females of the tribe in the darker corners of the village. Even this diversion (if I could believe Pablo) was part of the natural Arwacan hospitality—which is to say that your Indian host, after he has provided you with bed and board, deems it only proper to provide a bedmate as well from his stock of wives.

But this is by the way, and, even had I been fancy free, I was far too exhausted to consider such diversions. After we had posted a guard and rounded up our amorous comrades, I was all too glad to collapse on a pallet of woven grass in one of the larger huts and drop into a dreamless slumber.

CHAPTER XV

Lluvia de Oro

I HAVE said that my sleep was dreamless—and so it was, until the night was far advanced. Then, as I often had on this grueling journey, I dreamed that I was in London again, on my pallet in the sewing room, and that my love was in my arms. This night, however, the dream was different. In a twinkling Susanna's sweet face had become Elvira's, and her kitten's purr had changed to a tiger's roar.

I wakened, cold with sweat, to find I was not alone, but my terror vanished in a breath when I saw that my visitor was only one of the headman's wives. She had been sent to comfort me when I was heard to cry out in my nightmare. In the end I was forced to summon Pablo, and to part with two strings of beads, before I could convince her that I wished to sleep alone.

The overlord of the village had been absent on our arrival, having gone to a peace council with a rival tribe which the Arwacas had recently vanquished, to arrange for the ritual surrender of plunder and wives. Gorged as he was on his return with the success of that mission, and more than a little tipsy from palm wine, he was generous when it came to selling us vessels for our journey, and enough food to last us until we could reach Morequito.

Our sea dogs, adept at handling most craft, needed little practice before they could manage the flimsy sailing *canoas*. Equipped with one or more lateen sails, these light boats could skim like swallows with the wind, but were apt to prove skittish in tacking. However, so great was the expanse of the Orenoque that we soon grew adept enough at ship handling, and decided to set our course for the Caroni.

Before we had been afloat an hour, we had learned to utilize the shallows along either bank (where the tug of the current was far less ardent), and how best to dodge the numerous sand bars. Now and again, of course, we were forced to sail boldly into midstream. The river, a sleepy brown snake only half conscious of its strength, rippled with hidden energies and sent our fleet dancing wildly to the four corners of the compass—but with each sortie we gained a bit more knowledge. Sometimes, with the wind in our favor, we could skim upstream hours on end.

That night (not knowing the nature of the country on either bank) we moored our little fleet in midstream, where a wedge of palm-studded islands offered a welcome bivouac, high above the suck of the current. On the second day we found that the landscape was changing rapidly as we forged above the area of the rain forest and into the kind of park-like savannas that surrounded our Trinidad roadstead. Here the country seemed even finer, rolling in great, grassy undulations toward the distant mountains. Wild pigs were everywhere, and more than once we surprised a herd of grazing deer at the water's edge. At noon, when we moored at a sand bar for our midday meal, we found that the place was a turtle hatchery, and feasted on the new-laid eggs, which Pablo roasted in the coals of our campfire.

It was at this halt that we had our first brush with enemies, an encounter that was both unexpected and bizarre.

Gross had gone ahead to chart our course (the captain of the *Lion's Whelp* was an experienced cartographer, and he had marked down every turning of our inland voyage). As usual, he had taken three other *canoas* with him, sending them ahead to test the thrust of the current and the depth of the channel, and jotting down markers on both banks to speed our return journey. At this point the river took an abrupt turn to the south, so that our fellow voyagers were lost to view before we could put our remaining craft in the water. When we heard a single shot, and then the fusillade that followed, we could not have been more startled had a full-sailed galleon swum into view on the great, sun-flecked stream.

The battle (if such a grandiose word is appropriate) ended abruptly in a few sporadic musket bursts. Silence greeted us as we swept round the bend and saw our boats clustered on the southern bank. The smoke of the muskets still drifted in the breeze when we fetched the shore, in time to see Gross drag the last of six dead Spaniards from the underbrush and tumble the corpse on the spongy grass. Here, seeming oddly unafraid in the circle of muskets that ringed them, were three Indians—looking at us with brown liquid eyes that asked forgiveness in advance.

"Tell me this, Raleigh," said our second-in-command. "Why are the dons afraid to surrender to Englishmen?"

These were the first dead Spaniards I had seen in my short lifetime, and the sight was hardly a pleasant one, though I knew them to be our mortal enemies. Our charting expedition, it seemed, had come upon them without warning. The sight of six white men, in this untracked backland, had been startling enough even before they opened fire.

Apparently the dons had expected no mercy from us, since they were hopelessly outnumbered and had no possible retreat. Fortunately their first scattered shots had gone wild. Gross, replying instantly with twenty muskets, had wiped out the party almost on the first volley. The Arwaca guides (scattering like frightened birds at the first flare of gunpowder) had returned to the riverbank to offer themselves as voluntary prisoners when Gross and his men had come ashore.

The victors' booty, we discovered, was on the meager side. Evidently the Spaniards were on their way downstream. All six of them were scurvy fellows, with only their absurdly scissored beards and their jaundiced skin tone to advertise their nationality. Save for a few well-gnawed joints of venison and the inevitable pots of rice, their *canoas* were bare as Job's cupboard. A single item rewarded our forage—an Indian basket containing tools for refining gold. These included a phial of quicksilver, saltpeter, and other reagents used for the trial of metals. In the very bottom of the basket (concealed by a false panel which my knife pried loose) was a tiny bag of gold dust.

Pablo and Tivi (each speaking his own language) questioned the Arwaca guides. Raleigh listened to the former's report with a stony countenance, though I could see that he was not too displeased by the results of today's hunt. Unlike myself, Sir Walter had seen his share of fallen foes and learned to take the facts of death in stride.

"Do they come from El Dorado?"

"No, *jefe*. These men were prospectors, exploring the backlands."

"Whence came the gold, then?"

"They washed it from a stream bed a day's sail upriver. Their findings were disappointing. They needed a week or more to sluice out this tiny bag." Pablo spread his hands in a quick gesture of dismissal. His mind (steel-sharp, for all its primitive origin) had already sensed the disappointment in Raleigh's countenance. "The Arwacas are from a village far downstream. They were preparing to return there, since their search was fruitless."

"Do the Spaniards have ships on the Orenoque?"

"No, señor. Only the sailing wherry in which they came. They planned to return to Margarita."

Raleigh shrugged, and turned away from the dead bodies, with an order that they be searched forthwith. It shocked me a little to note his total absence of pity. At the same time I could see that pity would have been wasted on these wretches. After all, they had fired the first shot. Had positions been reversed they would have cut us down without compunction.

The search revealed no additional clues—save that the leader, one Carlos Morales, held a lieutenant's rank under the governor of Margarita and had been granted a leave of absence to go adventuring on the Guiana coast. The dons had made several attempts to penetrate the mysteries of this tropical heartland, all of them pusillanimous, most of them doomed in advance. Morales' commanding officer would hardly be surprised if his lieutenant failed to emerge from the jungle, nor would he be likely to investigate his absence. The Orenoque had claimed its share of victims since its discovery. I could not help wondering if the Caroni would prove more hospitable.

While we were finishing our business on the riverbank, De Vera fidgeted like a man possessed. A dozen times, it seemed, he had gone through the prospectors' basket, running the gold dust through his fingers and urging (in two languages) that we continue our journey upstream. In spite of Pablo's report, he obviously expected to bark his shins on nuggets before the day's end.

"Let the sons of *putas* lie," he urged. "Can't we press on?"

Raleigh gave him a withering glance. "Surely you'd grant fellow countrymen Christian burial?"

"The vultures will see to that—or the *lagartos*."

The light in the man's eyes, at that moment, was something I could willingly have spared myself. Gold fever is a monstrous disease, and I had reason to know that it attacked aristocrat and commoner alike. Elvira's suitor was a nabob, to the manner born. At this moment, while he slavered over that pinch of gold dust, he seemed only a greedy beast of prey.

"El Dorado has awaited us for nearly a hundred years, Señor de Vera," said Captain Gross. "It'll wait awhile longer —until we've prayed for the dead."

De Vera shrugged, and returned to his place in my *canoa*, where he continued to sulk as we unlimbered spades from another vessel. It took a sharp command from Raleigh to bring him ashore again, and he continued to swear under his breath as he performed his share of the grave digging. We needed pick-axes as well as spades before we could fashion a trench deep enough to protect those six carcasses from the wild beasts of the region. Raleigh read the burial service as the last spadeful of earth was tossed into the trench. Finally we placed a cairn of stones above it and sank a rude cross at its head. Then, with our consciences secure, we released the three Arwaca guides, wished them Godspeed on their down-river voyage— and, with all sails spread, resumed our drive for Morequito.

All that sun-bitten afternoon we nursed every scrap of wind as we quartered the current in search of slack water. When the breeze died with evening we made a second camp on a sand bar in midstream. Tivi had warned us that we were approaching the boundary of his domain and might run afoul of hostiles on the morrow.

Raleigh sat aloof from the company (with his charts on a camp table, and his thoughts elsewhere) while we settled for the night. When he summoned De Vera with a curt gesture, I could guess how heavily our noontime adventure was weighing on his thoughts. Naturally I was at his elbow before he fired his first question.

"Tell me this, Don Felipe," said my mentor. "Why did you shed no tear for your countrymen today?"

"I've no grief left for fools, Señor Raleigh. They should have surrendered at once, since your force was clearly superior."

"Do you believe this region will one day be part of Britain?"

"I'm a man of affairs, señor, not a fortuneteller," said the Spaniard. "Don't ask me to read the future. At this moment, I'm on the scent of gold."

Raleigh opened the miners' kit and weighed the bag of gold dust in his palm. "Would you call *this* the key to El Dorado?"

De Vera shrugged. "At least it is a signpost."

Sir Walter smiled thinly. "Your prospectors were not too thorough, despite their portable laboratory. Captain Gross has tested this dust. It's poor stuff indeed—what our London jewelers call fools' gold."

The Spaniard took this information with aplomb. I was positive that he felt it was a lie. "Since you're our leader, sir," he said carefully, "I won't dispute your findings. But I still believe El Dorado and Manoa are not too far beyond. And since you continued to set a course upstream, you must agree."

"You know our purpose," said Raleigh. "First we plan to establish our claim to Manoa. On the return journey we mean to bind the caciques in a firm treaty with England. I've baubles enough to make friends of the savages, and stout lads who'll stay on as the Queen's ambassadors until she can possess this region in fact as well as name. Aren't you a little concerned—now we're moving into what your King claims as his territory?"

"Not if I'm granted my share of the gold," said De Vera. *"Our* empire is already established. Yours is still a thing of charts and pious proclamations. I think we'll outlast you, señor."

Raleigh rolled an eye in my direction. The look convinced me he was baiting De Vera to force the Spaniard into stating his credo—if he possessed one. "I'm assuming you've come this far in good faith," he said. "What if our mission ends in failure?"

"That is my gamble," said De Vera calmly. "If we reach Morequito, you will find me useful. If Manoa lies beyond, I'll trust you to provide my marriage settlement. So far, I refuse to look beyond."

"Then you don't share your King's passion for keeping New Spain inviolate?" I asked.

"So far," said the Spaniard, addressing Raleigh rather than me, "we've outstripped you in the New World. It's my guess we'll continue to do so tomorrow. You English will never be colonizers."

"Why, Señor de Vera?" asked Raleigh.

"Kindness is your curse. Even if you did lay claim to Guiana, you'd never hold it, because you treat these red devils as humans. *We* have never made that mistake. To us, they are mere beasts that serve our need."

"Even beasts can devour their masters," I reminded him.

"Not if the master keeps the whip hand." Again he did not deign to notice me directly. "Take the three guides you released this afternoon. In your place I'd have shot them on the spot rather than permit word of this expedition to go down river."

"But that would be murder," I protested.

"So it would, in your language." This time he gave me a glance heavy-lidded with contempt. "For the English the villain is always a Spaniard. Why should I disappoint you by failing to conform?"

"Have you never thought of Indians as fellow men?" asked Sir Walter.

"Sir Walter, the Spanish are the dominant race in the New World. They must remain so. As I've said, you English will never be colonizers if you continue to treat your captive peoples easily. A man who fears death at your hand will always serve you. Those who know only kindness will knife you for your pains."

"The philosophy of master and slave," said Raleigh. "You

have stated it accurately. It will end by destroying the whole Spanish empire—no less surely than it destroyed the Romans."

"We've already flourished here for a century."

"Flourished is hardly the right word," said Raleigh. "All you've really done is build a few seaport fortresses, founded on gold—and gold alone. Do you remember Midas and his magic touch? Believe me, it can kill as well as cure."

"Yet you seek El Dorado no less ardently than I."

"Only to fill my sovereign's coffers and convince her this land must be part of England."

"So be it," said the Spaniard. "Who am I to dispute a leader's word, when I am only here on sufferance?"

He left us on that, at a nod from Raleigh, and rolled himself in the heavy blanket he called a poncho. In another moment he was snoring lustily—dreaming, no doubt, of the treasure that awaited him upstream. For my part, I sat by the fire long after my comrades had also composed themselves for sleep. The emotion I felt at this moment was a blend of hate and fear, and an aversion I could not put into words, though it resembled the loathing I felt at my first sight of a venomous snake.

In the days that followed, De Vera proved a willing shipmate, though he was scarcely a friendly one. Our principal difficulty (where he was concerned) was his obstinate desire to explore every creek mouth on the voyage to Morequito, in the hope that its streaming mud flats might yield gold. Now and then, when we were forced to halt and replenish our stores, Raleigh found it necessary to put him under guard, lest he wander into the jungle and lose his way.

I will not detail the vicissitudes of that long voyage upriver. Suffice it to say that we avoided the hostiles of whom Tivi had warned us and reached the next important Indian village in safety, the town of a powerful cacique named Toparimaca. This headman, a true potentate in the great Carapana nation, received us with extreme civility as the ambassadors of the English Queen. He also provided us with an escort of a dozen war *canoas,* that we might pass in safety through the country of the Aroras, a race of Indians almost black in color, who made war with poisoned spears and arrows. Five days' sail beyond his domain and we were in the land of Morequito—

the chieftain who had given his name to the town near the mouth of the Caroni.

Here, at our first great objective, we found that Morequito had died only a few months before. The name of Bartolomeo de Vera had lost some of its luster in the interval, since the Indians (with the illogic of primitives) had somehow blamed his demise on the Spaniards' visit. Indeed, so great was their animosity, we were forced to conceal the true identity of his kinsman, and passed De Vera off as one of us.

The present cacique, a man named Assapona, professing to be a hundred and ten years old, received us civilly when he found that our intentions were peaceable. Once again we were showered with food and other gifts, after we had arranged for the purchase of a fleet of barges for our strike up the Caroni. We were also obliged to attend a nightlong banquet, washed down with a strange (and devilishly potent) herb wine seasoned with peppers, which set one's throat afire even as it expanded the heart.

Next morning, with heads still addled by that burning potion, we began our assault on the Caroni. At first view it seemed a formidable stream, but we found that the *canoas* could breast its current once we had entered it. The barges, however, were worse than useless. On the third day of our ascent we were forced to moor them in a cove, since the denseness of the forests along both banks made towropes impractical.

Assapona had told us that our journey up the Caroni would end at a great waterfall, beyond which not even a *canoa* could advance—not that this mattered greatly, he added, for Manoa itself lay just above the falls. The ancient cacique's eyes had gleamed while he described the Seven Cities of Gold and the princes who ruled them. El Dorado, or the Golden One (the name is untranslatable in the native tongue), had been part and parcel of his tribal folklore for generations.

If we could believe his story, the original golden man—probably an Inca prince escaping from the tyrannies of Pizarro—had captained a mighty host that had invaded the country above the falls. They had settled there in the reign of Assapona's father, founding their empire on its incalculable riches. As for the Golden Ones (if, indeed, they were corporate beings and not the epitome of man's longing), we were told that the rule had passed from father to son. Their power over the people and their wealth was absolute, and their skins were invariably gilded to distinguish them from their subjects.

I had heard the legend in England in almost exactly the form it was repeated to us by this savage chieftain. All that I can now add, by way of personal postscript, is the record of our own discoveries as we drove down the last miles to the headwaters of the Caroni.

We could hear the cataract a whole half day before we glimpsed it, so dense was the tunnel of green through which we paddled, now that the Caroni had dwindled to a swift-flowing stream. All that afternoon the banks had grown constantly steeper, for we were now in the piedmont of the great central mountain ranges sketched in so vaguely on our charts. When we made camp—in a bosky dell whose trees shut out the view ahead—the air was almost cool.

Because of the high banks, we had had no use for our sails. At times the narrowing stream had roared like a millrace. More than once we had been forced to make portages around it. Now, tired as we were, we dropped into an uneasy slumber, haunted by the thunder of the cascade. When we were roused by the first hint of sunrise we saw that the wind had shifted in the night, blowing its spray into our dell, until the treetops sparkled with rainbows.

It was a bare half mile to our journey's end.

One by one, our *canoas* debouched into a foam-flecked basin directly beneath the falls. Our first view of the waterfall was breath-taking. The watery column seemed to tumble from the sky, so dense were the mists that covered the escarpment from which it roared. Then, as the vapors lifted, we saw that the cliff was perhaps two hundred feet in height, a thing of tortured granite faults and steep, brush-filled ravines that lifted to the sheer rock face just below the top.

The waterfall was broken into two parts. The first drop, which coincided with the naked cliff itself, was no more than forty feet, a roaring cascade that smoked down into a shallow basin in the midst of those tumbled granite masses. The second drop, by far the greater, was more mist than water, a shining, lacy apron that seemed to hang between earth and sky until it showered into the pool where our flotilla rested.

We beached our *canoas* in silence while we continued to stare at this magnificent freak of nature. At that precise moment the sun rose above the jungle barrier and struck the cliff with an arrow of radiance. In a twinkling the ghostly cascades changed from white to copper, from copper to pure gold. I heard Raleigh gasp beside me—and felt the echo of that gasp in my own throat. In sober truth, I had never seen a thing more beautiful.

De Vera was the first to speak. For once, he echoed our thoughts.

"*Lluvia de Oro,*" he said hoarsely. "A true rain of gold. Pray it's a good omen, gentlemen."

So far as we could tell from below, there was no sign of human habitation above the falls. If the descendants of the Incas were spying on us from that granite battlement, they remained invisible, though we scouted all possible approaches to the cliff, in the vain hope that we would uncover a trail, or, at the very least, some evidence that ours were not the first footfalls to disturb this virgin solitude.

Shortly before noon Raleigh called a halt to our futile scrambling. While some stood guard, we seized the opportunity to cleanse ourselves in the pool—plunging to its crystal depths, or daring to stand in the pelting of the cascade itself. Even then, we did not relax our vigilance. Try as we might, we could not escape the conviction that someone was peering down at us, from that jungle-choked escarpment.

"Well, Shawn?" said Raleigh, when I stretched out beside him on the sun-warmed grass. "Must we storm El Dorado head on?"

"There seems no other way, sir."

"Will you risk it—now you've had your rest?"

"I've climbed in Ireland," I said. "Say the word, and I can reach the top within the hour."

Raleigh shaded his eyes against the glare. "So far as I can judge, these battlements continue indefinitely. 'Tis a perfect barrier between their world and ours."

"So perfect, it isn't even guarded," I agreed. "Do you truly believe Manoa lies beyond?"

"I've come a long way to test that belief," he said. "Prove I'm right, lad, and there's nothing I won't give you."

"We'll need ropes for that last forty feet."

"Take what you like, Shawn, but set out at once. I'll want your news by nightfall."

"Will you accompany me, sir?"

Sir Walter looked down at his right knee, which he had twisted during yesterday's portages. "Were I your age," he said, "I'd have lost this stiffness overnight. Today, it would never take me to the summit. Choose whom you like for your companions. Or, if you prefer, ask for volunteers."

"Pablo and I can make the ascent between us."

"Suppose you encounter enemies?"

"It's a chance we must take. We could never hoist men-at-arms up that rock face."

We shook hands on that and moved to rejoin the others, most of whom were still bathing in the pool. "God be with you, Shawn," he said. "Bring me what news you can, and bring it soon. My patience is nearly gone."

In the end, to my vexation, De Vera insisted on accompanying us. The Spaniard, by his own account, was a practiced climber. With a great windmilling of his arms and shouted oaths, he also maintained that it was his right to ascend to the threshold of El Dorado and see, with his own eyes, whether an approach was feasible by this route. All of us understood him perfectly, of course. The fellow had never trusted us and he was sure we would play him false today. In the end Raleigh gave in with a shrug, and the three of us set out around the margin of the pool, toward the first of the steep ravines that angled upward to our goal.

Since I had been appointed leader of the climb, I sent Pablo ahead to cut a path with his cane knife, and instructed the Spaniard to keep a safe ten paces behind, lest he be harmed by falling rocks. Bringing up the rear, with a fair interval between us, I was thus able to keep De Vera constantly in view. It amused me to see how closely he inspected each rocky outcrop, as though he expected to claw out gold with his fingernails. Burdened as we were with ropes, pickaxes, and iron spikes, we could hardly have borne the added weight of saber or musket, so we carried no arms. As I had told Raleigh, we must run the risk of meeting enemies en route.

More than once, as we continued our precarious approach to the pool that divided the two cascades, I was forced to shout orders to De Vera, who was forever pausing to test promising boulders with his pickax. Had our amateur prospector succeeded in dislodging one of these rock masses, he might well have crushed me. With each panting step we took, the way grew steeper. Soon we were creeping rather than walking

—and using hands as well as feet to support us on a slope that was merging with the cliff itself.

Still, thanks to the dense vegetation that sprouted between each granite outcrop, there was purchase enough to make the climb more painful than hazardous. Now and again, by taking advantage of a fault in the rock, we were able to zigzag nearer to our objective, smoking like a vast caldron overhead as the cascade thundered down, and sending an aurora borealis of rainbows into the brilliant afternoon.

Throughout this portion of the climb we had been careful to work well to the left of this pool, since the rock in its vicinity was a mass of lichens, and slippery as glass from constant drenching. Twenty minutes after we had left ground level, Pablo put aside his cane knife and stood erect on a narrow ledge that was just above the upper pool. When De Vera and I scrambled to his side he passed the rope back to us and instructed the Spaniard to knot it firmly about his waist. We followed this example in turn, until we were roped together as securely as a trio of calves on their way to the butcher's. Only then did Pablo venture to approach the pool.

Viewed at this level, the basin was far smaller than the one below. Hollowed by the endless pounding of the cataract, it was roughly oval in shape, and channeled into the lower waterfall through a score of mouths. The cliff down which the water poured beetled slightly above our ledge. To my chagrin, I realized that we should have ascended on the right of the falls—since the escarpment on that side, though equally sheer, was accessible through a vast fissure that opened halfway to the summit. Fortunately the erosion of centuries had worn a kind of moon-shaped cave under the cataract itself, so that it was a simple (if ticklish) matter to work our way behind it.

Watching De Vera closely, I saw him go pale as Pablo tugged on the rope and dodged nimbly through the hissing white veil; then his backbone stiffened, and we followed the Indian's footsteps. Once inside the cave, we found that we could see nothing until our eyes adjusted to the translucent bath of sunlight visible through the cascade. The footing was solid (though each of us slipped more than once as we worked toward the far side, and the very rocks seemed to tremble from the impact of the falls). In a space of minutes we had stepped through another wall of mist and stood safely on the far side of the pool, in clear view of our anxious comrades below.

Seen close at hand, the fissure that had looked so accessible a moment ago was revealed as no more than a natural fault in the rock, enlarged by some earthquake long ago. Here and there in its crumbling inner surface were spurs of rock to give us handholds of sorts as we attacked the last, and most dangerous, part of our climb. Elsewhere, save for a few grass tufts and a wind-tortured tree just below the summit, the cliff was naked as a fresh-laid egg. I was grateful that Pablo had begun to scramble upward without even pausing for breath—and warned myself not to look behind me as I dug in behind the Spaniard's boot heels.

The fissure took us to within twenty feet of the top before it petered out. For the balance of the climb we were forced to work our way step by step—chipping holes for the spikes and anchoring them with a sharp blow of the pickax, then belaying a second rope on these anchors, up which we hoisted ourselves, hand over hand, like circus acrobats scornful of their lives. Steel-muscled as we were after our long fight with the river, we had the strength for this joint-cracking work, so long as we kept our minds from the ground two hundred feet below us. Once, De Vera dared to glance over his shoulder. I saw the sweat pearl his forehead and feared he would faint then and there, before he forced mind and energies back to the task at hand.

The last few feet of our ascent brought us below the wind-twisted pine. Pablo tossed a coil of rope across this natural anchor and tested the caliber of its roots with a few vigorous tugs before he trusted his weight to it. In another moment he had hoisted himself to the safety of the summit. De Vera came next, with an assist from the Indian. Then I lifted my own wildly swaying body, hand over hand, until I was close enough to anchor arms and scramble up beside them.

Our friends below were cheering, but the wind whipped the sound away. From that height they seemed unreal as two-legged ants dancing on a sunlit carpet. When I let my eyes rove down the skein of ropes below us I felt a wave of vertigo and leaned hard on Pablo's arm until the giddiness passed. To restore my equilibrium, I turned my gaze to the far horizon, across the rainbow-bridge of the *Lluvia de Oro*. The brown-green jungle we had traversed seemed endless from this van-

tage point, broken only by the silvery ribbon of the Caroni.
Despite the crystal light of afternoon, I could only guess at
the location of Morequito and the greater river on which it
stood.

There was something in that emptiness that chilled the
heart, even as it cleared the mind of mists. Fighting our way
up its river, aware of nothing beyond the next sand bar, we
had been but dimly aware of the immensity of this land called
Guiana; nothing had mattered except the hand blistered by
hours at the oars, the dull ache of hunger when bad weather
had spoiled a noontime meal, the release of sleep. Here, for
the first time, I could gauge the depth of our explora-
tion—and measure our puny effort against the wilderness that
hemmed us.

"Sangre de Cristo!"

The oath brought me back to my companions. De Vera was
standing with arms akimbo, ignoring the country we had traversed for the landscape that lay beyond the cliff's edge. On
his far side, Pablo gave a shrug and a downdropping quirk of
the lips I would long remember. Between them, my partners
in the ascent had prepared me before I risked a glance in turn.

Looking back on that moment now, I cannot say what I expected from the land called Manoa. Man's earthly paradise
takes many forms—and, since man's reach must always ex-
ceed his grasp, it is a landscape whose colors are constantly
shifting. In my dreams I had pictured white castles with roofs
of gold, guarded by captains in golden armor. If those battlements scraped the sky and their guardians were nine feet tall,
I had only my errant fancy to blame. At other times, I had
been sure that the region mistakenly called El Dorado would
bristle with enemies, that its treasures would be guarded far
more jealously than man's honor or woman's virtue. Both
moods had taken conquest for granted. How could it be otherwise, with Raleigh as our leader?

What I glimpsed that afternoon was all the more heart-
breaking in the light of those aureate visions. I can see now
that the discovery was inevitable, but wisdom and dream had
not kept pace on that unhappy afternoon. Item for item, the
country we now faced was even more menacing than the region we had just quitted.

At our feet, sweeping almost to the horizon's rim, was a
noisome fen, filled with the war of birds' wings and weeping

from every muddy pore. Constricted on both sides by the granite escarpment we had just scaled, it drained off, in some measure, through the waterfall. Neither man nor beast could have forced a path through that evil swampland. Beyond, boxing the whole southern horizon, was a wall of saw grass; farther still (a blue shadow whose contours I knew by heart) the jungle began again, empty and mysterious as it had been since Adam's fall.

If the Incas had dwelt here once, there was no artifact to mark their presence. Indeed, I have since had good reason to believe that some cataclysm of nature had created this boggy desert before the dawn of history, and that it had resisted human penetration to this day.

De Vera spoke first, breaking the silence that reality had imposed on romance.

"We can advance no farther," he said. "Even an Englishman can see that——"

"I'm going to make sure," I said and started toward an island in the swamp, where a palm tree thrust its branches skyward. Even in that short distance we could feel the gumbo suck at our boot tops before we stood in its shadow.

I had shucked my jerkin; it needed only a thrust of my shoulder to deny De Vera the right to be the first witness of our failure. After our scramble up the cliff, the hole of the palm tree seemed easy enough. In a matter of minutes I was squatting in its crown. The view that opened before me was only a confirmation of our first estimate.

At this height, the swamp (and its sullen backdrop of jungle) seemed never-ending. Later I would learn that we were standing on the watershed separating the valleys of the Orenoque and the Amazon, sister rivers that bled the land mass of New Spain in their special fashion, and spurned the visitations of man. The knowledge would have been small comfort had I possessed it today. But I knew De Vera was right when I slid to earth again—much as it pained me to endorse his judgment.

"See for yourself," I said. "Raleigh will want your report as well as mine."

The Spaniard swarmed up the palm bole as I turned to Pablo. "Did your nephew come this far?"

"Only in his mind, señor."

"It was a dream then—and nothing more?"